BY
Steven Banks

ILLUSTRATED BY Mark Fearing

HOLIDAY HOUSE · New York

HOLIDAY HOUSE is registered in the U.S. Patent and Trademark Office.

Printed and bound in October 2019 at Toppan Leefung, DongGuan City, China.

www.holidayhouse.com

First Edition

10 9 8 7 6 5 4 3 2 1

Library of Congress Cataloging-in-Publication Data

Names: Banks, Steven, 1954– author. | Fearing, Mark, illustrator.

Title: Middle school bites / by Steven Banks ; illustrated by Mark Fearing.

Description: First edition. | [New York City] : Holiday House, [2020]

Series: Middle school bites ; #1 | Summary: Eleven-year-old Tom Marks has

big plans for middle school, but the day before classes begin he is bitten

by a vampire, a werewolf, and a zombie.

Identifiers: LCCN 2019003951 | ISBN 9780823445431 (hardcover)

Subjects: | CYAC: Middle schools—Fiction. | Schools—Fiction. | Vampires—Fiction.

| Werewolves—Fiction. | Zombies—Fiction. | Humorous stories.

Classification: LCC PZ7.B22637 Mid 2020 | DDC [Fic]—dc23

LC record available at https://lccn.loc.gov/2019003951

ISBN: 978-0-8234-4543-1 (hardcover)

To my brother, Alan,
who knows that both monsters
and middle school can be scary
and fun.—S. B.

You are not going to believe this happened.
I wouldn't believe it either.
I would think you were lying or crazy.
But it all *really* happened.
I promise.
Just *look* at me.
See?

1.

Horrible Beginnings

I got the first bite when I was asleep in bed at 2:54 in the morning.

I got the second bite three hours later as I was running down a dark road in the woods.

I got the third bite that afternoon in an old, abandoned carnival trailer.

It all happened on the second-worst day of the whole year. The last day of summer vacation. The next day I was starting middle school. There were four reasons I was excited to go to Hamilton Middle School and four reasons I wasn't.

The 4 Reasons I Was Excited to Go to Middle School

#1 I wouldn't be a scrawny little elementary school kid anymore.

#2 Tanner Gantt would not be there. Tanner Gantt is a guy who bugged me all the time in elementary school. My name is Tom Marks and he always calls me Tommy Farts. He's big, and he shoves kids and calls them names and makes fun of them. He pretends to accidentally spill his drink on you and then he says, "I'm soooooo sorry!" He also throws food at people and puts people in trash cans. Nobody fights back because he would probably kill them.

But now I didn't have to worry about him anymore. My best friend, Zeke Zimmerman, had called me two weeks before school started.

"Tom!" he yelled on the phone, all excited. "Tanner Gantt is *not* going to Hamilton! He's moving away! He's going to Kennedy Middle School!"

This was the best news ever. But I have to admit, I sort of felt sorry for the kids at Kennedy.

#3 I would get my own locker. I could keep all my school junk in it and put up cool pictures and stash emergency food. I could keep secret stuff in there too. I didn't have any secret stuff yet, but I might someday.

I was a little worried about forgetting my locker combination.

My sister, Emma, who is sixteen and my second-least favorite person in the world (Tanner Gantt is number 1), said to me, "If you forget your combination, you have to

pay the grumpy janitor a hundred dollars
to open your locker . . . and the principal
announces to the whole school that you
forgot it."

I imagined sitting in class and hearing
over the loudspeaker: "*Attention, students
and faculty, this is your principal! Tom
Marks forgot his locker combination. Don't*

forget to laugh and point at him all day.
Thank you."

I decided to write the combination on the bottom of my shoe in case I ever forgot it. I found out later that Emma was lying. She does that ALL the time.

#4 Annie Barstow is going to my middle school. She's eleven, the same age as me. She's smart and funny, and I like the way her hair looks. I hoped that someday Annie would be my girlfriend, but I was going to wait until we were in high school to ask her about it. We'd just be friends in middle school. I called this *The Girlfriend Plan*. I think it's a good idea to make plans.

If Annie agreed to be my girlfriend, then, after high school, we'd go to college together, then maybe we'd get married and get really, really rich and live on our own private island. I didn't know how we were going to get rich. I was counting on Annie to figure that out because she's so smart.

I haven't told Annie about *The Girlfriend Plan*, yet.

The 4 Reasons I Was **NOT** Excited to Go to Middle School

#1 They give you a TON of homework.

Last year Emma warned me. "The books in middle school weigh twenty pounds each. Some kids get so much homework that they break their backs carrying books home."

"No way, Emma," I said. "You're lying."

Then she pointed out the window at a kid walking down the sidewalk. He was wearing a back brace.

"There goes one now," she said, smiling.

I later found out she was lying.

Emma is the worst.

#2 Finding my seven different classrooms and getting to them on time before the tardy bell rings.

"One time a kid got lost trying to find his classroom," said Emma, "and they *never* found him."

She is *such* a liar.

#3 There might be some brand-new bullies at Hamilton School who could be even worse than Tanner Gantt.

"Oh, there totally will be," said Emma with a smile.

#4 They force you to run four laps—a whole mile—in Phys Ed around The Biggest Track in the World. I hate running.

I knew middle school wasn't going to be easy, but I was prepared because I had a plan. I called it *The Invisible Tom Plan*. I was going to be quiet and stay in the background and not get noticed. That way I wouldn't get bullied or get a dumb nickname for doing something stupid and embarrassing.

One time, a kid at my elementary school was giving a report about hot dogs. He was really nervous, so he kept saying "dog hots" instead of "hot dogs." From then on everybody called him Dog Hots.

One little mistake and your whole life changes.

My whole life changed on the day before I started middle school.

2.

The First Bite

I always go to Gram's house the last weekend before school starts. She lives out in the woods about three hours from my house.

Gram is pretty old, but she doesn't act old. She rides a mountain bike and hikes and does yoga. She has long gray hair, and always wears blue jeans, colorful shirts, wire-rimmed glasses, and crazy necklaces. I think she used to be a hippie.

Gram has a lot of vinyl records at her house, that she sings along to. She plays them super loud.

"That's because she's losing her hearing," says my dad.

Gram says, "If you don't play rock-and-roll loud, why play it?"

On my last day at Gram's—the day before school started—I had set my alarm to go off at six o'clock. I had decided to get up early and go running to get in shape, so I could do those stupid four laps in Phys Ed. It's like they want you to be in the Olympics. I don't want to be in the Olympics.

But I also don't want to be the loser guy coming

in last, huffing and puffing and looking like I was going to faint. So, I'd been getting up early to run. This was my second day. I probably should have started about two weeks ago, but I *hate* running and getting up early.

Since I ran early, before the sun came up, it wasn't hot. I didn't want to get all sweaty and disgusting. Who likes to get all sweaty and disgusting? Probably the same people who want to be in the Olympics.

That morning, I turned my alarm off and looked out the open window. I could see the moon through the trees. It was about three-quarters full. That's when I felt something weird on my neck, like a bite. I remembered feeling something on my neck in the middle of the night and brushing it away and going back to sleep. I *always* get bit and

stung by things at Gram's house. I even made a list that I keep on her refrigerator.

It's like the first bug that sees me arrive at Gram's house tells the other bugs that I'm there. "Hey! Guys! Look! Tom's here!"

"I *love* to bite that kid!"

"Me too! I bit him five times last year!"

"Oh, yeah? I stung him ten times!"

"No you didn't!"

"Yes I did!"

"You're a bee! If you sting him one time, you die!"

"Well...um...I... *wanted* to sting him ten times."

THINGS THAT HAVE BITTEN OR STUNG TOM MARKS

FLEAS
MOSQUITOES
BEE
HORNET
WASPS
YELLOW JACKET
TICK

"Hey! Let's have a contest to see how many times we can bite and sting Tom!"

"That is an awesome idea!"

"Attack!"

I know that doesn't *really* happen, but it feels like it does.

I thought the bite on my neck was a spider bite, but it turned out to be something a million times worse.

○ ○ ○

I put on my running shoes, some sweatpants, and a T-shirt. I was kind of tired because Gram and I had stayed up late the night before watching a movie.

After we had eaten dinner—homemade pizza and root-beer floats—she leaned across the table and whispered, "You want to watch a scary movie?"

Gram *loves* scary movies.

The one we watched was pretty old and in black-and-white. I thought it was going to be boring, but it was actually pretty scary—and funny too. It had Frankenstein and Dracula and the Wolfman in it, chasing these two guys named Abbott and Costello. I have to admit, I might have closed my eyes a few times. I hoped Gram didn't see me do it. But I knew that even if she did, she wouldn't tell anybody.

○ ○ ○

When I came downstairs, Gram was in the kitchen making her coffee. She gets up early every day even though she doesn't have to.

"Good morning, Tommy! Ready to go running?"

She's the only person that I still let call me Tommy. Everybody else calls me Tom. (Well, except

Tanner Gantt, who calls me Tommy Farts, but he doesn't count.)

I showed her my neck. "Is this a spider bite, Gram?"

"Let me take a look."

She looked at my neck. "I don't see anything— wait.

There's two tiny little red dots. You must taste so good, he bit you twice."

She wrote "spider" on the list on the refrigerator.

o o o

I went out the back door and down a path to the road. It takes longer, but I didn't want to walk by Stuart.

Stuart is Gram's neighbor's ginormous dog that is always tied up in the front yard on a rope. He's a Siberian husky, with gray-and-white fur so he looks like a wolf.

"Stuart" was the worst, dumbest, most ridiculous name for that dog. He should have been named Brutus or Killer or Max.

Stuart always barks at me when I walk by.

When I was five, Emma said to me, "If Stuart ever chews through his rope, you'd better run, because he will chase you and bite you and kill you and eat you."

I didn't want to find out if she was lying.

o o o

It was still pretty dark out, but the moon made enough light to see as I ran down the dirt road. I'd been running for about five minutes when I came around a corner and stopped dead in my tracks.

Stuart was standing in the middle of the road.

He must have finally chewed through his rope and decided to wait out here to attack me. (I hate it when Emma is right about stuff.) He tipped his head back and howled. I'd never heard Stuart howl before. On the scary scale of 1 to 10, it was a 9.

He lowered his head and looked right at me, growling.

"Stay," I said. "Stuart . . . *stay*."

I didn't know if he would actually stay, but it was worth a try.

Slowly, I started walking backward.

"Good dog. . . . Stay. . . . Staaay. . . ."

He didn't stay.

Stuart started running right at me. Now I wished I *had* wanted to be in the Olympics and had been training since I was five years old, so I could run super fast.

He was getting closer. I turned around and started to run as fast as I could. "Stay! . . . Sit!" I yelled over my shoulder. "Roll over! . . . Play dead!"

He was right at my heels now, trying to bite me. I could hear his jaws snap together every time he tried and missed. I was getting tired and I knew I couldn't keep running this fast.

Why did I get up to run? Who cares if I was the loser guy in Phys Ed class, huffing and puffing and fainting when we had to run the mile? Now I was going to get bitten by a giant dog who couldn't do any tricks.

Stuart bit me on my ankle. I felt his teeth go through my sock and into my skin.

All of a sudden I saw bright white lights shining ahead.

They were the headlights of a big truck coming down the road, right toward us. Stuart got scared and ran off into the woods. The truck drove by and I stopped running and bent over, with my hands on my knees, trying to catch my breath. I rolled up my pants leg and saw that the back of my sock had some blood on it. I pulled my sock down and saw the bite marks.

Was I going to get rabies?

Gram and I saw a movie about a kid who got rabies. He went crazy and started drooling white, foamy bubbles. It was pretty disgusting. I could just see myself on the first day of middle school, foaming at the mouth. People would call me Bubble Mouth the rest of my life.

Now I *wish* I had gotten rabies. That would have been so much better than what happened next.

o o o

Gram was on her front porch, doing yoga, when I ran up to the house.

"Gram! You're not going to believe what just happened!"

She untangled herself from the position she was in and smiled. "Try me."

"I got bit again!" I said, rolling down my sock to show her.

"What got you this time?" she asked.

"Stuart!"

Gram got *really* mad. I'd never seen her get that mad. Even at the TV news. She took out her phone and called her neighbor and started yelling at him. She said some words I had never heard her say before. I didn't even know she knew some of those words. She must have learned them when she was a hippie.

Then she stopped yelling and listened. Her face slowly got less mad looking. After a while, she quietly mumbled, "Oh, uh . . . well. . . . Sorry, Jasper. Bye." She hung up the phone, cleared her throat, and looked at me.

"Well . . . It seems that Stuart is at the veterinarian having some eye surgery. So, it must have been some other nincompoop's dog! Tommy, have you ever had a rabies vaccination shot?"

I hate getting shots.

"Uh . . . I think so—yeah. I have. Definitely. I don't need one. I'm good."

Gram grabbed her phone. "Well, just to be safe, let's call your mom."

She told my mom what happened and asked her if I'd ever gotten a vaccination. Then she hung up and turned to me. "Well, I guess you and I are going to the emergency room."

On the way out of the house, Gram went to the refrigerator and wrote "dog" on the list of things that had bitten or stung me.

∘ ∘ ∘

I sat next to a kid about my age in the waiting room. He had long hair that hung across his face, and he was staring down at his thumbs like they were the most interesting thing in the world. Gram was at the desk, talking to a nurse.

The kid held up his right thumb. "Dude. Doesn't this look broken to you?"

It looked normal to me, but it sounded like he wanted me to say it was broken.

"Yeah. It does."

He nodded and slouched down in his seat. "Why are you here?"

"I got bit by a dog. I've gotta get a rabies shot."

He shook his hair out of his face and his eyes got wide. "Rabies? Seriously? That sucks. My brother has a friend who has a cousin that got bit by a dog and he had to get five shots."

Five shots? Why would you have to get five shots? I only got bitten once.

"Really?" I said. "Are you sure?"

"Yeah! And the shots hurt wicked bad. They use, like, the biggest needle you have ever seen, and they stick it super far into your arm and they're like the most painful shots you can get."

He reminded me of Emma.

I hoped he was lying, or his brother's friend's cousin had made up the story, or he just liked to hang out in emergency waiting rooms and scare people. I could see Tanner Gantt doing that.

"Tom Marks?" said the nurse.

I stood up.

The kid shook his head. "I am so glad I am not you, dude."

o o o

The doctor examined the bite on my ankle, cleaned it, sprayed it with something that stung, and gave me some pills to take.

"These'll make you drowsy," she said. "You'll get a good sleep tonight."

I only had to take some pills? No problem. I could handle that. I knew that stupid kid was lying. The doctor smiled.

"Now roll up your sleeve, I'm going to give you two shots. You'll have to get another shot in three days. And then another shot after that in seven days, and *one more,* two weeks later."

Five shots.

That kid hadn't been lying.

I decided I was *never* going to go to Gram's again.

The doctor picked up The World's Biggest Needle.

"This might pinch a little."

I hate it when doctors say stuff like that. They're lying! Shots *never* pinch. They hurt. I wish doctors would just say, "Listen, kid, this is going to be extremely painful, because I'm going to jab this sharp, pointy thing right into your arm. Get ready to scream."

If I were a doctor, that's what I'd say.

I rolled up my sleeve, turned my head away, squeezed my eyes shut, and gritted my teeth. It didn't *pinch*. It hurt!

The doctor was washing her hands when Gram remembered the bite on my neck. "One more thing, Doctor? Can you check something on his neck?"

The doctor looked at my neck and smiled. "Well, I'm certainly glad you're getting the rabies vaccination shots."

"How come?" I asked.

"That's a bat bite."

3.

Rare and Bloody

We started the long drive back to my house. The sky was still gray and cloudy, and it started to rain. We stopped for lunch at this place we always go to called Billy Burgers. There's a statue on the roof of a skinny little kid taking a bite out of a giant hamburger that's twice as big as he is. One Halloween somebody stole the hamburger and replaced it with a dummy that looked like a real person. It looked like the kid was eating a man, who was screaming his head off. Gram loved it and sent me a picture.

As we walked through the parking lot, there was a girl with long red hair, a little older than me, holding a black cat over her shoulder. When I walked by, the cat went crazy and arched its back and started hissing and yowling at me.

The girl spun around and yelled, "What did you do to Mr. Waffles?!"

"Nothing!" I said, backing away.

She glared at me. "Yes, you did! Did you say something? Did you scare him?"

"No! I didn't do anything!"

She started talking to the cat. "What did that boy do to you, Mr. Waffles? Did he say something mean? Did he make a scary face?"

Gram looked at the girl and said, "Young lady, my grandson did *nothing* to your cat. And by the way, Mr. Waffles cannot understand a single word you're saying."

000

We sat in our favorite booth, right by the front window.

"What can I get you?" asked the waitress.

"Billy Burger and a Coke, please," I said.

"How you want that burger cooked? Rare? Medium? Or well done?"

I *always* have my hamburgers well done, but for some reason a rare hamburger sounded delicious.

"Rare, please," I said.

The waitress smiled at me and wrote on her pad. "That's the way I like 'em too. Nice and bloody. What size Coke?"

I don't know why, but I was staring at a vein on the side of her throat. She had a long neck and her skin was pale, so I could really see the vein.

She tapped my menu with the end of her pencil. "Hello? What size Coke?"

"Oh—uh, sorry," I said. "Super Mega." My parents NEVER let me get the Super-Mega size. Gram is the only person who does.

That rare hamburger was the greatest hamburger I ever had in my life. The Super-Mega Coke turned out to be one of my biggest mistakes.

o o o

We were in the car about half

an hour away from my house when I said, "Gram, I gotta go to the bathroom."

She smiled and said, "Didn't a wise old woman say to go back at Billy Burgers?"

I looked up "nearest restroom" on her phone and found one at a gas station off the highway. We turned down a long dirt road we'd never been on before, then up a little hill, and there it was. A creepy old gas station in the middle of nowhere. It was just a wooden shack, with three gas pumps in front of it.

I gulped. "Gram, this looks like that gas station in the movie we watched last summer, *Gas Station Maniac Massacre Part 2.*"

"It does!" she said. "That was a good one. Those teenagers stopped to ask directions from a scary guy wearing overalls, and then he ate them."

Gram stopped the car by the gas pumps, then got out and looked around. "I don't think it's open. I guess you'll have to do your business in the bushes."

I *did not* want to go in the bushes. I would have bet a million dollars that there were snakes, lizards, raccoons, rats, mice, and coyotes, all waiting there to bite me.

"What do you want?!" barked a voice.

We turned around and saw a skinny guy smoking a smelly cigar. *He was wearing overalls*. He looked like he'd been doing something that he didn't want anyone to know about.

Gram smiled at him. "Hello. My grandson needs to use your restroom. Where is it?"

Old Smelly Cigar Guy gave her a dirty look and said, "You gonna buy gas?"

"Yes. Just as soon as you move away from these gas tanks with your lit cigar, which could ignite them and blow us all to kingdom come."

Old Smelly Cigar Guy grunted and jerked his thumb over his shoulder. "Restroom's out back."

He glared at me as I got out of the car and said, "Don't you go poking around back there, kid. Do what you gotta do and get out."

I had no plans to spend one second longer than I had to at The World's Scariest Gas Station.

○ ○ ○

I walked around the building to find the restroom. I went by an old trailer with a faded sign on the side that said: **T. E. ROBBINS CARNIVAL OF ODDITIES**.

Past that was a broken-down merry-go-round for little kids. Some of the wooden horses were on the ground in the dirt. A few of them didn't have heads. This place was getting creepier.

You *don't* want to know what that restroom looked like or smelled like. I don't think anyone had cleaned it in about twenty years. I held my breath the whole time and went as fast as I could. I washed my hands but didn't dry them because I couldn't hold my breath any longer.

I was walking back to the car, wiping my wet hands on my pants, when I saw a smaller trailer, like the kind people tow behind their cars. It had a faded sign on it.

People must have paid to go into the trailer to see one of the carny people dressed up like a zombie.

The door to the trailer wasn't closed all the way, so I peeked in. I could see something in the back corner.

So I went inside.

I used to wonder why people in movies went into scary-looking houses or creepy rooms or spooky closets or dark caves, when they *knew* something bad was inside. I don't wonder anymore, because I did the same thing. You just *have* to see what's in there.

It was a dummy, in raggedy, torn clothes, with a zombie mask, tied to the chair with a rope. I moved closer to get a better look and stepped on something. It was a bunch of old, greasy Billy Burger bags. Who would want to eat in there?

The zombie mask was amazing. It had long, stringy white hair and gray skin and seriously messed-up teeth. You could see part of its brain through a hole in the side of its head, and one of its eyeballs was hanging out.

The skin on the mask looked super realistic. Almost like real human skin. I leaned in closer, so I could touch it and see how it felt. That's when the zombie leaned forward and opened its mouth.

4.

Tricked

I threw my hands up in front of my face. I *might* have let out a little scream too. The zombie mask had super-realistic, disgusting, rotting teeth and they scraped the bottom of my hand.

I ran out of there so fast.

I figured I must have stepped on a switch that made the dummy move. Or Old Smelly Cigar Guy had followed me out there and pushed a button to make the dummy lean forward and scare me. He probably did that to people all the time. I have to admit, I probably would too.

Gram had finished getting the gas. Old Smelly Cigar Guy wasn't there. I bet he was inside, looking out a window and laughing at me. I jumped in the car.

"Everything okay, Tommy?" asked Gram, looking concerned.

"Yeah. Let's go."

I looked down at the bottom of my left hand. There was a little cut with some blood where the zombie dummy's teeth had grazed me. I wiped my hand on my jeans.

After we got back on the highway, I took another one of the pills the doctor had given me, so I didn't get rabies and turn into Foamy Bubble Mouth Guy.

Gram put on some of her old music. It was a girl singing about being seventeen years old and all the depressing things that happened to her. She had a soft, pretty voice, and I got sleepy listening to it.

All of a sudden, I heard my mom yelling, "Wake up, Middle-School Man!"

5.

Not Looking Good

Bam! Bam! Bam!

My mom was knocking on my bedroom door. I looked at my clock. It was 7:00. I sort of remembered getting home, stumbling in half-asleep and talking to my parents about the bite on my neck and the dog bite. I didn't say anything about cutting my hand on the zombie dummy. Then I went right to bed.

"Get up! Get dressed!" Mom yelled in her happy voice. "It's the big day!"

"Okay, Mom," I mumbled. "I'm awake."

I heard her walk away down the hall humming. Why was she so happy? I bet she wasn't that happy the day *she* started middle school.

I sat up in my bed. I felt weird. I wasn't exactly sick, but I didn't feel normal. Maybe this was how everyone felt on the first day?

The other weird thing was that I noticed my house smelled super intense. I could smell Mom and Dad's coffee downstairs. It smelled like they had opened a Starbucks in the kitchen.

I could also smell my sister Emma's perfume.

She must have used two gallons for her first day of tenth grade, thinking all the boys would fall in love with her. No one would ever fall in love with Emma unless they were crazy.

I could even smell Muffin, our dog—who smelled like he needed a bath. He could have used some of Emma's perfume.

I'd been planning what I was going to wear on the first day of school. It was part of my *Invisible Tom Plan*, so nobody would notice me.

First Day of
School Clothes

Regular Jeans
Plain Blue T-Shirt
Gray Hoodie
Black Adidas Shoes
White Socks

After I got dressed I was so hungry it felt like I hadn't eaten in a week. I ran downstairs to the kitchen.

Mom was at the sink, with her back to me, mixing a disgusting, healthy fruit-and-vegetable drink in the blender. "How you feeling, Tom? Nervous? Excited?"

Dad didn't look up from his iPad, where he was reading the news.

"I was a little nervous on my first day of middle school," he said. "So I pretended I was a secret agent, working undercover at the school, looking for an evil genius disguised as a teacher who was going to take over the world."

Emma, who was looking at her cell phone—which she does twenty-four hours a day—shook her head and said, "That is the lamest thing I have ever heard."

"Where's Gram?" I asked.

Mom poured her gross health drink into a glass. "She left really early this morning, so she wouldn't hit traffic. She had a dance class to get to. She said to tell you 'good luck at school.'"

Emma finally looked up from her phone. "Wow. You look *awesome* this morning, Tom. You are a seriously handsome dude. You are going to have so many girlfriends at Hamilton."

Emma NEVER compliments me. She hasn't said anything nice about me since I was three years old. She was being sarcastic. One of her favorite things to do.

Mom gave Emma the stink eye. "Emma Gwendolyn Marks!" Then she looked over at me. "Tom, you *do* look a little pale."

"Gram *always* makes us put too much sunscreen on," said Emma.

Mom made her worried face. "And you've got dark circles under your eyes."

"Gram probably let him stay up late to watch a scary movie," said Emma.

Dad looked up from his iPad. "Your eyes look a little red and watery."

"I bet you forgot to take your allergy pills." Mom sighed. "You *have*

41

to take them when you're up at Gram's. There's ragweed all over the place."

Emma did a big, fake smile. "But seriously, Tom, I *love* what you're doing with your hair."

I immediately knew there was something wrong with my hair. I reached up and touched it. Weird. It felt a little thicker and a little longer.

"When was the last time you washed it?" asked Mom.

"Or used a comb?" said Emma.

"You need a haircut," said Dad.

Emma looked away from her phone (which *never* happens). "Okay. Guys? Let's just admit it: Tom is strange looking. Can we accept that fact and get on with our lives?"

Emma always tries to be funny, but she isn't. I wish there was a place where you could trade in your sister if you didn't like her and get another one. Or better than that, get a cool older brother. I would go there so fast.

"Hello, Mr. Marks! Welcome to the Trade-In-Your-Sibling Store. What may I do for you?"

"I'd like to trade in my sister, Emma, for a brother."

"Ah, yes! I've heard about your sister, the in-famous Emma Marks, a cruel, despicable,

evil creature if ever there was one! Well, today is your lucky day. We've just got in a new shipment of awesome older brothers and I have the perfect one for you! Tyler, will you come out here, please? Ah, here he is! Tyler, this is Mr. Marks."

"Hey, man, my name's Tyler. You wanna get some pizza, hang out, play some video games, tell me all your problems so I can solve them and have me beat up any bullies who are bothering you? Oh, and hey, here's a hundred bucks I don't need. Take it."

"He's perfect! I'll take him!"

"Splendid, Mr. Marks! We'll send our people over to pick up Emma. Of course, no one will want her, she's what we call one of 'The Untradeables.' So, we'll just sell her for scientific experiments."

I really wish there was a place like that.

o o o

I brushed my messy hair back with my fingers to flatten it down.

Emma squinted her eyes at me. "When did your ears get pointy?"

"My ears aren't pointy!" I touched the tops of my ears. They felt different.

"Your grandfather had pointy ears," said Dad. "Girls *loved* him. They called him Elfy."

I did NOT want girls calling me Elfy.

I got up and went to the mirror in our hallway by

the front door. Emma uses it about a million times a day. I looked in the mirror, but I couldn't see myself very well. My reflection was blurry and dark.

"Hey! What's wrong with this mirror?" I yelled.

"You're looking in it!" yelled Emma from the kitchen.

"I can't see anything!"

"You're lucky. You don't want to see yourself this morning!"

"Stop it, Emma!" said Mom.

"That mirror is just dusty," said Dad. "Clean it!"

"Tom!" yelled Mom. "Come eat something! You're going to be late for school!"

Everybody talking about how weird I looked had made me forget I was starving. I went back in the kitchen.

"Mom, can you make me some scrambled eggs and bacon and hash browns and sausage and toast and pancakes? And maybe some French toast and waffles? And a milkshake?"

Mom laughed. "You're kidding me."

I wasn't kidding.

"Did Gram not feed you this weekend?" said Emma as she texted on her phone.

"I don't have time to make all that," said Mom. "And you don't have time to eat it. Have some cereal."

Dad smiled. "I was *always* hungry when I was your age."

I poured myself a giant bowl of Frosted Honey Nut Cinnamon Flakes. I had just put the milk in when Muffin came through the doggie door. Our dog is a real mutt, about ten different breeds mixed together. He loves everybody. If a person tried to rob us, Muffin would just wag his tail and watch them take our stuff.

"Hey, Muffin," I said.

He trotted toward the table, but all of a sudden,

he froze. He lowered his head, and the hair on his back started to rise up. Then he did something he'd never done before.

He growled at me.

Everybody looked up. Even Emma.

"What's the matter, Muffin?" said Mom. "It's just Tom."

I growled back.

I'd *never* growled at Muffin. Or anyone. Even Emma.

"Tom, stop that!" said Mom.

Muffin put his tail between his legs and slinked out of the room.

Emma glared at me. "What is wrong with you?"

"Muffin growled at me first!" I protested.

"Just hurry up and eat," said Mom.

I started wolfing down the rest of my cereal. It was soggy now. Yuck.

Mom glanced out the window and sighed. "It's so dark and gloomy. I don't think the sun is going to come out today."

"I *love* this kind of weather," said Emma, who was going through a "dark and gloomy" phase. All her clothes and her hair and her fingernails were black. She even wanted to get black contact lenses, but my parents wouldn't let her.

"Make sure you both take an umbrella," said Mom.

There was no way I was taking an umbrella to school. Who did Mom think I was? Mary Poppins? Middle-school kids don't take umbrellas to school. Well, at least the cool ones don't. You wouldn't see Jason Gruber, who was good at every single sport ever invented, with an umbrella. Juan Villalobos, who played guitar and looked like he should be on TV, would never have an umbrella. Annie Barstow *might* take an umbrella, but it would be a cool one.

The only kid who would definitely take an umbrella was Abel Sherrill. He was the weirdest kid in our elementary school. Abel wore a suit and tie and carried a briefcase and brought an umbrella to school—*every single day*. Kids made fun of him at first, but he didn't care. Eventually they got used to him. I wondered how Abel was going to do at middle school with all those new kids who'd never seen him before.

A car horn honked outside.

"That's Pari," said Emma. "I'm outta here."

Pari Murad was Emma's best friend. I don't know why Pari hangs out with her. Pari is the complete opposite of Emma. She's nice and smart and polite and pretty and a human being.

Emma and I grabbed our backpacks and started to walk out of the kitchen. Mom blocked us in the doorway. "No one leaves this house until they brush their teeth."

My mom is obsessed with teeth. She should have been a dentist.

"I'm gonna be late!" said Emma.

"Me too!" I said.

"Maybe," said Mom. "But you won't have any cavities."

Emma and I both stomped up the stairs to brush our teeth.

"And don't forget to floss!" yelled Mom.

I couldn't see myself very well in my bathroom mirror either. Did I need to get glasses? When I was flossing, I noticed that two of my side teeth,

on the top, looked different. I touched them with my finger. They felt kind of pointy and a little longer than they used to. Or were they like that before? I don't pay that much attention to my teeth. I hoped I didn't have to get braces. If I had to get braces *AND* glasses, I would seriously think about being home-schooled.

○ ○ ○

How weird is it, that one day those two teeth would scare people, get me in trouble, *and* save my life?

6.

Disappearing

Emma and I finally headed out the front door.

Mom grabbed me and hugged me. "You are going to have the greatest year!"

"Okay, Mom!" I said. "Will you stop hugging me so I don't miss my bus!"

"Have fun at school, Emma," said Dad.

Emma did a fake smile. "I will! Because *everybody* has fun at school! It's the funnest place in the world!" Then she rolled her eyes.

"Wait!" yelled my mom. "We've got to take the picture!"

Emma tipped her head back, closed her eyes, and opened her mouth. For a second, I thought she was going to howl. She just said, "Nooooo!"

Mom was digging in her purse for her phone. "Yes! We have to!"

"No, we don't!" said Emma.

Ever since kindergarten, Mom has taken a picture of Emma and me on our front porch on the first day of school. You can't fight it. You just have to give in and do it. One year, Emma refused to and Mom started to cry. Emma let her take the picture.

"Here it is!" said Mom, holding up her phone.

"Hurry up!" said Emma.

"C'mon, you guys, smile," said Mom.

"I am *so* not smiling," said Emma.

I didn't feel like smiling either. "Mom! I don't want to be tardy on my first day!"

"You are going to *love* having these pictures someday," said Mom. "One, two, three!" She looked at her phone and made a face. "That's strange. I can't see Tom."

Emma rolled her eyes. "*When* are you going to learn how to use the camera on your phone?"

For once Emma was right. Mom is *always* accidentally putting in weird colors and effects when she takes a picture. I looked at the picture. There was Emma, who looked like she was

competing for The Most Unhappy Sixteen-Year-Old Girl in the World Contest. And winning. But I wasn't in the picture. There was just a blurry, sort-of-empty space. It was like I was invisible.

"I erased Tom," said Mom.

"Good!" said Emma.

"How did I do that?" moaned Mom. "I *hate* this new phone! The old one was *so* much better!"

"Later," said Emma as she walked to Pari's car.

"Hi, Tom!" yelled Pari as she waved at me.

"Hi, Pari!" I tried to wave back, but it was difficult because I was trying to get out of Mom's second death hug. She is much stronger than she looks. Just before Emma got into Pari's car, she turned around and looked at me.

"Good luck at middle school, Tom."

I couldn't believe she said that.

"Uh. Thanks, Emma."

She smiled. "You'll need it."

o o o

Pari and Emma drove away with music playing really loud. But not as loud as Gram plays it.

Mom held up a small, brown paper bag. "Here's your lunch."

"Mom! *Nobody* takes their lunch to middle school!"

"Who says?"

"*Everybody!* I wanna buy my food in the cafeteria."

She handed me the bag. "Tomorrow you can buy your lunch. It's your favorite. Salami-and-cheese sandwich, an apple—*please* eat it, don't throw it away—chips, and Oreos."

I wanted to eat it right then. That big bowl of soggy Frosted Honey Nut Cinnamon Flakes hadn't filled me up.

Why was I so hungry?

7.

No More T-Man

I ran the two blocks to the bus stop. I was hoping that no one at school would notice my crazy hair, my watery eyes, my pale skin, my two weird teeth, and my sort of pointy ears. I pulled my hoodie farther down over my face.

My best friend, Zeke Zimmerman, was already at the bus stop. I've known Zeke since kindergarten. I accidentally spilled a whole jug of blue paint on him the first day. Most kids would've gotten mad or socked you or told the teacher. Zeke just laughed. He thought it was the funniest thing in the world. He walked around the class, covered from head to toe in paint, saying, "I am Mr. Blue! Who are you?"

We've been best friends ever since.

"T-Man!" he yelled when he saw me.

He calls me T-Man. I don't really like it, but once Zeke starts doing something it's hard to make him stop. But I couldn't let him call me T-Man now that we were going to middle school.

"Hey, Zeke. Listen, I need you to stop calling—"

"First day of middle school! We are going to be so cool!" shouted Zeke as he jumped up in the air and pumped his fists. "Yes! Yes! Yes!"

"Okay, Zeke. Calm down," I said quietly. I have to tell Zeke to calm down a lot. He gets excited about everything. "Listen to me. We're in middle school now, so we've gotta act like middle-school kids."

Zeke nodded. "I totally hear you, T-Man!" Then he threw his backpack up in the air and caught it.

"And *don't* call me T-Man anymore," I said.

Zeke looked at me like he was going to cry. He's a pretty emotional kid. "But . . . but . . . I've been calling you T-Man ever since kindergarten."

"Yeah. I know. And that's why you need to stop."

He looked down at his shoes and quietly said, "Can I call you T?"

"No."

"Can I call you Mr. T?"

"No!"

"Can I call you The T-ster?"

"NO! Just call me Tom."

"Okay. . . . Can I call you T-Man when it's just you and me?"

I knew this was the best I could hope for with Zeke. "Yeah. I guess. But *only* then."

"Excellent!"

As I turned to see if the bus was coming, my hoodie slipped off of my head.

Zeke looked at me and said, "T-Man! What happened?"

8.

Glasses and More Bad News

I started to explain to Zeke. "My gram put too much sunscreen on me, I didn't take my allergy pills, I inherited pointy ears from my grandfather, and—"

"No, dude! Not that!" he said, his eyes getting bigger.

"What?" I asked nervously. Had I grown a horn on my head?

Zeke got about an inch away from my chin. "You've totally got a pimple!"

I felt my chin. There was a little bump. I hadn't noticed it.

"Oh, man," said Zeke. "I can't wait till I get my first pimple!"

Only Zeke would say something like that.

I told him about the bat bite and the dog bite and the zombie dummy.

"Excellent!" he said.

Zeke always says "excellent" when he likes something. It's his favorite word.

"Too bad a radioactive spider didn't bite you!" he said. "You could've turned into Spider-Man!"

He was being totally serious.

"Uh, Zeke," I said, "you do know that Spider-Man isn't real, right?"

He smiled and said, "Well, I know that we haven't *seen* a real Spider-Man . . . yet!"

He started doing jumping jacks. Zeke does that randomly sometimes. I have no idea why. I asked him once and he said, "Sometimes you just have to do jumping jacks."

The bus came down the street toward us.

"Stop, Zeke," I said. He always stops when I

tell him. "Okay, remember: We're not elementary-school kids anymore. I told you about my *Invisible Tom Plan*. And no more 'T-Man.'"

Zeke saluted me. "I totally hear you . . . Tom."

It sounded really weird when he called me Tom.

○ ○ ○

We got on the bus. I knew some of the kids, but a lot of them were from other schools or they were older kids in the higher grades. It's kind of unfair. You're the cool, older kids in elementary school, at the top of the heap, and then two months later, you start middle school and you're the dorkiest, youngest kids at the bottom of the barrel.

I noticed I could smell what every single kid had in their backpacks. Plenty of peanut butter sandwiches, cheese sandwiches, granola bars. I was so hungry, I felt like I could eat everything.

"Welcome, gentlemen," said the bus driver. "My name's Esperanza, but you can call me Bus Lady." She looked like she might be a professional wrestler in her spare time. "Take a seat, any seat."

Bus Lady gave me a weird look and started fiddling with a little silver cross on the necklace she was wearing. All of a sudden, I didn't feel so good. We walked past her down the aisle, and I felt better.

Luckily there weren't very many kids on the bus yet. We headed toward the emergency-exit row. That's the best row to sit in on a bus because there's more room.

Halfway down the aisle a girl looked up and smiled at me. She had short hair and glasses and was wearing jeans with holes in them on purpose.

"Hey," she said.

"Hey," I said, and kept walking.

Then Zeke said, "Hey, Annie!"

I had just walked past Annie Barstow.

I hadn't recognized the person who I hoped would be my future girlfriend *and* wife *and* business partner. Annie looked *totally* different. She used to have super-long hair and she didn't wear glasses and she never wore jeans with holes in them on purpose.

Annie looked at me and tilted her head to the side. "You look kind of . . . different."

"I think I could say the same thing to you." I thought that was a cool thing to say.

Annie shrugged. "Yeah. I cut my hair and got glasses."

She looked good in glasses. Some people do, and some people don't. I guess it depends on the kind of glasses they get. It was going to take me a while to get used to her short hair.

"You look kind of pale," said Annie. "Do you feel okay?"

Zeke jumped in. "His gram put too much sunscreen on him, he didn't take his allergy medicine, his grandpa had pointy ears, and look, he's got his first—"

"What teachers do you have, Annie?" I quickly said, before Zeke started telling her about my first pimple.

"Sit down," she said. "I'll show you."

Annie moved her backpack off the seat next to her. There was an umbrella sticking out of it. The handle was in the shape of a person's hand. It was cool looking. Of course.

Zeke had plopped down in the emergency-exit row. He was looking at me with a "Why aren't you sitting with me?" expression on his face. There was no way I was not going to sit next to Annie, though. I was just about to sit down when I heard a voice that I thought I would *never* ever hear again for the rest of my life.

"Hey, look! It's Tommy Farts!"

I turned around and saw Tanner Gantt getting on the bus.

9.

The Backpack Toss

How had this happened? Tanner Gantt wasn't supposed to be here! He was supposed to be going to Kennedy Middle School and torturing *those* kids. Zeke told me that he had moved across town and was going to live with his father.

Why do I ever listen to Zeke?

Tanner Gantt walked toward me with a smile on his face. As he came down the aisle, he punched one kid in the shoulder, rapped another kid on the top of his head with his knuckles, and knocked a book out of a third kid's hand.

"Ow!"

"Hey!"

"Quit it!"

Tanner Gantt looked like he had grown even taller and bigger and meaner over the summer. He still had his short black hair and his dark eyes, though.

I could tell *exactly* what Tanner Gantt had eaten for breakfast from his breath. A super-chunky peanut butter sandwich on toasted white bread, and a Dr Pepper. That sounded delicious.

He was staring at me. "Man, you need to get some sun. And what's up with your eyes? You been crying? What's the matter, baby? Is Tommy Farts scared to go to middle school?"

"Ignore him, Tom," said Annie.

Tanner Gantt turned toward Annie and stared at her. "Barstow? Why'd you cut your hair?"

"None of your business," said Annie.

"And you got glasses. Too bad. You used to be almost pretty."

I started to say "Shut up," but I only got out "Sh—" when I stopped. You'd have to be *insane* to say "Shut up" to Tanner Gantt. I had actually said "Shh," which was less insane, but still not a great idea.

Tanner Gantt looked at me like he was going to kill me or eat me.

Bus Lady was looking in her rearview mirror at us and yelled, "Find a seat and sit down!"

Tanner Gantt turned to her with a big, fake smile and said, "I'm sooo sorry, ma'am."

He took a step toward me. I was seriously thinking about jumping out the bus window to escape.

"Let me help you with your backpack, Farts."

He grabbed my backpack and threw it all the way to the back of the bus. It could have been worse; at least he hadn't thrown me.

○ ○ ○

I always thought that Tanner Gantt would end up in prison when he grew up. I had a plan for when that happened. I call it *The Tanner Gantt in Prison Plan*. I was going to walk by his prison cell window once a week and yell, "Hey, Tanner! How's prison?"

Then he would look out his window and start crying and say, "Tom! Help me! It's horrible here! I hate it! I wish I'd never called you names and threw food at you! *Please* tell the warden I'll be good and never do anything bad again!"

Then I'd yell back, "I'm soooooo sorry, Tanner! I'm just too busy today. I have to drive my super-fast, million-dollar sports car back to my big mansion on my private island and go swim in my giant swimming pool and play video games on my humongous TV! See you next Wednesday!"

Then I would walk away to the sound of Tanner Gantt crying.

Or there was the possibility that he'd love being in prison. He'd be with people exactly like him who'd teach him how to do more bad stuff, and they'd all have a great time.

o o o

After he threw my backpack, Tanner grabbed Zeke's arm and yanked him out of the emergency-exit row. "Move it, Butt Brains, this is *my* seat!"

Tanner Gantt had never called Zeke Butt Brains before. I wondered if he had come up with that over the summer. He usually called Zeke other names, like Butt Eyes or Butt Ears or Butt Mouth or Butt Head or Butt Dork or Dork Butt. Tanner Gantt really liked the word "butt."

Zeke and I walked to the back of the bus. We sat down in the last row, and the bus started to move. I was *still* starving. I took out my lunch bag and ate my salami-and-cheese sandwich. Tanner Gantt turned around and looked at me.

"Hey! Look! Tommy Farts is so stupid that he doesn't even know it's not lunchtime yet!"

I wanted to walk up the aisle, pick up Tanner Gantt,

and throw him out the bus window. It was weird. I almost felt like I could do it.

∘ ∘ ∘

The first thing we did at school was line up for locker assignments. My locker was number 104, and the combination was 76-54-72. It was on the first floor near a bathroom. I sat down on a ledge and was just starting to write my combination on the bottom of my shoe when I looked up. There was a kid with his back to me, putting *HIS* junk in *MY* locker. He had on a black jacket, matching black pants, and shiny black shoes.

"Hey! That's my locker!" I said.

The kid turned around.

It was Abel Sherrill. The Weirdest Kid at Anybody's School. He was, of course, wearing a black suit and tie and carrying a briefcase, and had an umbrella hooked over one arm. It smelled like he'd had an omelet with cheese, onions, and bacon, an English muffin, tea, and fresh-squeezed orange juice for breakfast.

"Greetings, Mr. Marks," he said with a smile and a voice that sounded like he was about thirty years old. "It appears that we shall be sharing a locker."

Abel calls everybody by their last name. It's always "Mr. Marks" or "Ms. Barstow" or "Mr. Zimmerman." He held up a piece of paper with his name on it and the number 104.

"Hey, Abel," I said, trying not to sound like I was mad that I had to share a locker with the last kid at school I wanted to share it with. Except maybe Tanner Gantt. That would have been worse.

Abel held up one of those things on a string that people hang from their rearview mirror so their car doesn't stink. It looked like a pumpkin.

"I purchased an air freshener to eliminate any unpleasant odors that might accumulate," he said. "I will change it periodically according to the season. This is called *Granny's Pumpkin Pie*."

He hung it on one of the hooks in the locker that should have been mine. Everything I put in there was going to smell like pumpkin pie. I don't like pumpkin pie. I didn't want my books and everything else I put in my locker to smell like that.

Abel tipped his head back and looked up at the ceiling. "Precipitation seems imminent. Glad I have my bumbershoot."

I didn't know what Abel was talking about. I found out later that "bumbershoot" was an old-time name for umbrellas. Abel uses a lot of words that nobody's heard of.

He looked at me closer and raised his eyebrows. "Are you feeling out of sorts? Under par? Not up to snuff?"

"What?"

"Are you ill, Mr. Marks?"

"No. I'm fine."

"Splendid!" said Abel. "Now I must dash off to first period. Be seeing you!"

He reached out to shake my hand. I didn't want to shake his hand, because other kids were looking at us, but I did. As soon as his hand touched mine, his expression changed. He stopped smiling and got serious.

He leaned forward and whispered, "Your secret is safe with me, Mr. Marks." Then he walked away, whistling. I didn't know what he was talking about—again. Abel is the weirdest kid I've ever met. And now I had to share my locker with him.

Sharing a locker turned out to be the least of my problems.

10.

The Worst First Day of Middle School That Any Kid Ever Had

First period was English. I sat right next to Annie. The seat was by the windows, and the sun had finally come out a little and was shining on my desk. As soon as I sat down I felt like I was burning up.

Did they have special windows at middle school that made the sun hotter for some reason? Why didn't anyone tell me this? I bet Emma knew, but didn't tell me on purpose. I had to find a seat across the room that wasn't in the sun.

Our English teacher, Mr. Kessler, told us we

had to read *five* books this year. I wasn't paying too much attention, because I was thinking about what seat to move to. When I sat down, it got dark and cloudy again so none of the seats were in the sun.

Annie raised her hand. "Mr. Kessler? I've already read all those books." She pulled a big, thick book out of her backpack, which looked like it weighed twenty pounds. "I'm reading *Moby Dick* now. Can I keep reading that?"

"Yes," said Mr. Kessler. "But you still have to give reports on the others."

"Gotcha!" she said.

If anybody else said "Gotcha!" to a teacher, they'd probably get in trouble. Annie never did. I don't know why.

The first book we had to read was *White Fang*. On the cover was a picture of a dog in the snow howling at the moon. It looked like the dog that bit me. The bite on my ankle started to itch.

Things were about to get weird.

o o o

Second period was Science. The teacher was Mr. Prady. He kind of looked like Ben Franklin, because he was sort of bald, but with long hair in the back, and he wore wire-rim glasses. He smelled like he had eaten a corn dog for breakfast. A corn dog sounded delicious to me right then. Five corn dogs sounded even better. I was starving. Abel was in the class, but luckily, he didn't sit next to me. I sat at a desk next to a shelf where there was a snake in a glass terrarium and a mouse in a tank. When I sat down, I noticed that they were both staring at me.

Mr. Prady started talking about the different experiments we were going to do during the year. Every time I looked over at the mouse and the snake, they were still staring at me. It started to creep me out.

At the end of class, Mr. Prady fed the mouse to the snake. One kid cried, one kid laughed, and one kid said he was going to throw up, but didn't. I got hungry again. I have to admit, I wasn't sorry to see the mouse go. Now only the snake was staring at me. I had a weird thought: I wondered what a mouse tasted like.

∘ ∘ ∘

Luckily, we had snack period next. I really wanted another rare hamburger, but they only had snack stuff. It was only ten minutes long. I barely had time to get in line, buy something, and eat it. I got a blueberry muffin and rammed it down. I looked around for Annie or Zeke but couldn't find them. I saw Abel and hid behind a post, so he wouldn't see me.

He saw me.

"Ah, Mr. Marks! I see you selected the blueberry muffin for your morning repast. I hope it's pleasing to the palate and sufficient to quell the old hunger pangs!"

Most of the time I had no idea what Abel was talking about.

He snapped the two latches of his briefcase, then opened it. He pulled out a roll wrapped in a cloth napkin.

"Croissant?" he offered, holding it out to me. "I rose at six o'clock this morning to make them."

It looked and smelled delicious, but I didn't want to stand there and eat it with him. Kids were looking at Abel, which meant they would eventually be looking at me to see who the weird kid was with.

"No, thanks," I said. "I gotta go."

o o o

Third period was History. I got a little bit lost getting there and ran in just as the bell was ringing. I sat down in the front row, a little out of breath, next to Dog Hots.

Dog Hots leaned over and whispered, "Don't call me Dog Hots, okay?"

I whispered back, "Okay."

But then I couldn't remember what his real name was.

Dexter?

Shane?

Jackson?

I had *no* idea.

Two girls from my old elementary school were sitting in the back of the class staring at me. Girls staring were better than a snake and a mouse. They were cupping their hands over their mouths and whispering to each other, but I could totally hear what they were saying.

"Does Tom Marks look different to you?"

"Yeah. He does."

"*Good* different or *bad* different?"

I didn't get to hear the answer because they stopped talking when the teacher, Mrs. Troller, started taking roll.

o o o

Fourth period was Math. The teacher was Ms. Heckroth. She had long black hair, was really tall, and never smiled once during class.

"In this class you will pay attention at all times," she said in a stern voice. "You will show up on time, ready to work; you will do your assignments; you will turn in your homework when due; and you will be prepared for tests. If you do these things, this class will be a pleasant experience. If you don't . . . it will be the opposite."

She pulled down a chart at the front of the room, and it started to roll back up. She grabbed it and cut her finger on the metal pull thing, and almost said one of the words Gram said when she was yelling at her neighbor. At the tip of her finger was a tiny spot of blood.

Then it got weird.

I could *smell* the blood.

And what was weirder was that it didn't smell bad.

It smelled . . . kind of good.

And then it got *super* weird.

All of a sudden, I got really thirsty.

11.

Dripping Paint

Fifth period was Art class. You get to choose two classes in middle school, and I chose Art and Choir because they both sounded easy. I wasn't worried about Choir. How hard is it to sing with a bunch of kids? But as far as art goes, when I try to draw stuff, it looks like a kindergartner did it.

I had a plan. I called it *The Easy Grade in Art Class Plan*.

Last summer Mom forced us to go to an art museum. There was a gigantic painting there by this guy named Jackson Pollock. It wasn't a painting of a person or a place or a thing. It looked like he had gone crazy and just poured and dripped paint all over the place. They had a video in the museum of him painting, and that is *exactly* what he did.

Mom said Jackson Pollock was an "abstract expressionist artist"—whatever that means—and the painting was worth over a hundred *million* dollars. I thought to myself, I could do a painting like that.

That's when I got the idea for my *Easy Grade in Art Class Plan*.

The art teacher was Mr. Baker. He was short and bald, and had a pointy nose. He kind of looked like one of the goblins that work at Gringotts Bank in *Harry Potter*.

"Today we are going to draw self-portraits with a pencil," he said.

I raised my hand. "Mr. Baker, I'm an abstract expressionist artist. Like Jackson Pollock. I don't draw. I drip and throw paint around."

I thought it would impress Mr. Baker that I knew the name of a famous artist.

"Oh, really?" he said as one of his eyebrows went up. "How interesting."

I was totally going to get an *A* in this class.

Then, Mr. Baker stopped smiling. "Today, Mr. Marks, you are going to be drawing a self-portrait with a pencil."

The Easy Grade in Art Class Plan wasn't working.

○ ○ ○

Mr. Baker gave everyone a mirror, a piece of paper, and a pencil. I had no idea what to do. I'm an abstract expressionist artist!

I looked in the mirror. It was blurry and dark. Maybe I had some rare eye disease where you couldn't see yourself very well in a mirror? I was definitely going to need to get glasses.

Since I couldn't see myself, my self-portrait ended up even worse than usual. The girl sitting next to me kept looking over at it and shaking her head. Her name was Capri and she had red hair. She could draw really well. Her drawing looked *exactly* like her.

My drawing could have been titled *Worst Self-Portrait Ever*. My face looked like a potato with hair on top. My ears looked like two slugs crawling up the side of my head. My nose looked like a bowling ball, and my teeth looked like piano keys.

At the end of class, Mr. Baker looked at my drawing for a long time. I thought he was going to give me an *F* or kick me out of the class.

"Is that how you see yourself, Mr. Marks?" he asked.

I didn't know whether to say yes or no. Was he trying to make a joke? Was it a trick question? I finally said, "Uh . . . sometimes."

"Very original," he said. "I like it a lot."

Capri gave me a dirty look. Mr. Baker hadn't said anything about her drawing.

The bell rang. It was *finally* lunch. I was starving again. But I had a major problem. I'd already eaten my lunch.

o o o

The cafeteria was big and noisy. Kids were sitting at long rows of tables, eating and talking and laughing, sometimes all at the same time. The food smelled amazing. I had told Zeke to meet me by the front door. He walked in, excited as usual.

"I am, like, having the best day ever!" he said. "Middle school is excellent!"

"I'm glad *someone's* having fun," I said gloomily.

Zeke said he'd share his lunch with me since I'd eaten mine on the bus. He got in line to get his food. I grabbed a table in the corner where nobody was sitting.

"May I dine with you, Mr. Marks?"

I looked up and there was Abel, in his three-piece suit, holding a tray, with his umbrella hooked over his arm. I looked around. Some kids were staring at Abel and pointing at him.

"Uh . . . sorry, Abel," I said. "I'm saving this table for some people."

"No problem at all, I shall dine elsewhere." He smiled and went off to another table. I felt a little bad about not letting him sit down, but the whole cafeteria would be looking at us, and that didn't work with *The Invisible Tom Plan*.

Zeke walked up with pizza on his tray. I love pizza. If I could eat pizza every day, I would.

"You can have half of my pizza," said Zeke as he sat down. "I'm not that hungry."

The pizza he got was called The Works. It had olives, peppers, sausage, pineapple, ham, bacon, and garlic on it. He held out half of the pizza to me.

Right away, I felt sick. It was like in one second, I had gotten the flu. All my muscles ached. I felt weak and had a headache. I felt like I was gonna puke.

I stood up. "I-I don't feel so good."

"Really?" said Zeke, with a mouthful of pizza. "I feel great!"

I ran toward the door and almost bumped into Annie.

"You okay?" she asked as I ran past her.

"Awesome!" I said as I banged the door open and ran outside.

I looked around for the closest bathroom, but I couldn't see one. I saw a trash can, but it was right next to a bunch of kids. If I had to puke into it and people saw me, I would be called Puke Boy or Pukey or Barf Boy for the rest of my life. But then, after I took a deep breath, I didn't feel sick. I started to feel a little better.

Until I saw Tanner Gantt sitting by himself on a wall eating his lunch.

12.

The Tanner Gantt Plan

I turned around as fast as I could. I started to walk away from where Tanner Gantt was sitting. I didn't think he had seen me. I was almost around the corner when—

BAM!

Something hard and wet hit the back of my head.

I looked down on the

ground and saw a half-eaten orange. I felt the back of my neck. It was all wet and sticky. I heard some kids laughing.

Tanner Gantt smiled and waved at me. "I'm soooo sorry, Farts! I was aiming for the trash can!"

There was no trash can anywhere near me.

o o o

I decided, right then, that if Annie and I ever got married and started our business and got rich, the first thing we would do is hire someone to throw food at Tanner Gantt *every single day* for the rest of his life.

Every day they would throw a different kind of food at him. Sometimes it would be a peanut butter sandwich with lots of sticky jelly. Sometimes a chocolate pie with lots of whipped cream. Sometimes nachos with a ton of cheese. The person that Annie and I hired would even follow Tanner Gantt when he went on vacation.

If he was at Disney World, taking a picture in front of the big castle, they would nail him with a chili-cheese hamburger.

If he was in Hawaii, surfing on a surfboard, they'd hit him with a sticky cinnamon roll.

If he was in Switzerland, skiing down a mountain, they'd get him with a hot fudge sundae.

And in New York City, if he was on top of the

Empire State Building—*BAM!*—pancakes with syrup.

"WHO KEEPS THROWING FOOD AT ME?!" he'd yell.

The person who threw the food would be amazingly good at hiding, so he'd never be seen.

"STOP THROWING FOOD AT ME!" Tanner would yell at the top of his lungs.

But the person would never stop.

Even if Tanner Gantt got married—which I seriously doubt he ever would, unless he found someone who was also a bully—our person would throw food at him at his wedding. He'd be all dressed up in a tuxedo, just about to say "I do." Our person would throw a big, giant plate of spaghetti and meatballs at him.

If Tanner Gantt lived to be a hundred years old, someone would still hit him with food every single day.

I would also have that person take a video every time he threw something. That way Annie and I could watch the videos on our island on our enormous, giant TV.

I bet we could hire Zeke to throw food at Tanner Gantt. We probably wouldn't even have to pay him. Zeke would do it for free. He hates Tanner Gantt as much as I do. Zeke could live in our guesthouse.

I found a bathroom and washed my neck off. I didn't have time to eat anything. The bell rang, and I had to go to sixth period: Phys Ed.

How was I going to run those stupid four laps around the track?

o o o

The good news was Zeke was in Phys Ed with me. The bad news was so was Tanner Gantt. When he saw me he said, "Can't wait till we start playing football, Farts. I am gonna smash you so hard."

We changed into our Phys Ed clothes in the locker room. That was weird. Let's just say there are a lot of different kinds of bodies.

I had practiced, over the summer, getting out of my regular clothes and into my gym clothes as fast as possible. My record was 12.4 seconds.

We also have to wear a jock strap, which is the most uncomfortable underwear ever invented. A kid told me they have surprise jock-strap inspection. You have to pull one of the rubber straps down, below your shorts, to show the coach you're wearing it. I thought about starting a petition to outlaw jock straps.

o o o

"Okay, ladies and gentlemen, we will be running four laps today," said Coach Tinoco when we lined up outside on the track. Coach Tinoco looked like the Hulk, except he wasn't green.

Luckily, it was still gray and cloudy, so at least I wouldn't get hot and sweaty. I was hoping it would start raining so we wouldn't have to run all four stupid laps.

"On your mark! Get set! GO!" yelled Coach. The fast people ran out ahead of everybody to show off. I ran next to Zeke and we talked. The first lap wasn't too bad.

"I hate jock straps," I said.

"Really?" said Zeke, surprised. "I've been wearing mine for a week—to get used to it. It's great!"

Coach yelled at us. "Pick it up, you two, or you'll have to run *five* laps!"

I ran faster. It was weird. I wasn't tired at all. I started passing people. I ran past Tanner Gantt, who got really mad. He tried to run faster and pass me, but he couldn't.

I even passed Jason Gruber, the fastest runner in school last year. He gave me a dirty look. Soon I was on the last lap, way ahead of everybody. Coach Tinoco was watching me. I couldn't believe it. I was going to be a track star! I *could* be in the Olympics! I'd get a gold medal and be on TV and be famous and make millions of dollars. Annie wouldn't have to think of an idea for how we would get rich.

Then the clouds parted and out came a bit of sunlight. All of a sudden, I got tired. I started to slow down. Jason Gruber passed me, with a big smile on his face.

I could barely move my legs. I had been an Olympic star, and now I was going to come in last place, huffing and puffing. I felt hot too, like I was burning up.

Tanner Gantt passed me and laughed. "Farts, you wimp!"

Zeke even passed me.

And then I fainted.

Do not *ever* faint in middle school.

o o o

I woke up in Coach Tinoco's office. He must've carried me inside. I think he thought I had died or something and he'd get in trouble. The school nurse came down and took my temperature. I was hoping she'd send me home, but no such luck.

"I think you'd better send me home," I said, trying to sound sick.

"What have you eaten today?" she asked.

"I didn't have any lunch," I said, but I didn't tell her why. "You can call my mom and she'll pick me up."

"Let's get some food inside you first," she said. She got the cafeteria to send down a barbecue beef sandwich and some milk. I felt better after I ate it.

For the rest of the day, whenever Tanner Gantt saw me, he would hold the back of his hand to his forehead and say in a high-pitched voice, "Oh no! I'm going to faint!" Then he'd fall down on the ground. He did this seven times.

He also started calling me Fainty.

I was so glad the day was almost over.

But one more horrible thing had to happen.

13.

Howl

When I left the coach's office it had gotten dark and cloudy again, and then it started to rain. While I was walking to seventh period, Abel suddenly appeared, out of nowhere, with his umbrella.

"Mr. Marks, may I offer you some protection from the deluge?"

It was raining pretty hard and I was getting wet, but I didn't want to walk to Choir class with Abel, in his three-piece suit, under his umbrella.

"No, thanks, Abel," I said. "I . . . uh . . . like to walk in the rain."

I hate to walk in the rain.

He smiled and left.

Choir was my last class of the day. It started out a million times better than the  others. I got to sit right behind Annie. The Choir teacher was Mr. Stockdale. He had a big beard and wore cool glasses. I decided if I had to get glasses, I would get glasses like his.

"Okay, singers!" he said, clapping his hands together. "I want to hear what you've got, so we're going to sing 'Home on the Range.'"

Some people groaned.

"I'm glad you approve of my song selection," he said.

I have to admit, I have a pretty good voice. I think I inherited it from Gram. Singing might be the one thing I'm good at. Annie looked around and smiled at me after we sang the first verse. The day was not going to be a complete disaster.

Then it happened.

I shouldn't have done it, but I did.

The chorus part was coming up. The part where

you sing *"Home, home on the range."* I decided to sing it really loud to impress Annie. I figured if I did this, after class she'd say, "Tom, you have an awesome voice! You want to do homework over at my house after school today? And have lunch together tomorrow? And go on dates in high school and go to the same college together and get married and start a business that I will think of (since you aren't an Olympic track star anymore) and live on an island and hire someone to throw food at Tanner Gantt every day for the rest of his life?"

I took a deep breath. I opened my mouth to sing "*Hoooome*" and instead . . .

I howled. I actually, honestly, totally *howled*.

○ ○ ○

Mr. Stockdale stopped conducting and glared at me. I thought he was going to throw his conducting stick right in my eye. Every kid looked at me and laughed. And it wasn't the kind of laugh where they think you're trying to be funny.

Annie gave me a look that felt like she was thinking, "I am never going to do any of those things you hoped we would do together."

"Was that supposed to be funny"—Mr. Stockdale looked down at his seating chart to see my name— "Mr. Marks?"

"No, Mr. Stockdale."

"This is Choir class. We sing. We do not howl. Do you know the difference between singing and howling?"

"Yes," I said, looking down at my feet.

"Good. If you do that again, you are out of my class."

○ ○ ○

When Zeke and I were about five years old we tried to make a time machine out of a clock, a vacuum cleaner, and some Legos. Obviously it didn't work. But if someone *had* invented a time machine,

I would've gotten in it right then. I would have gone ahead to the future, to the last second, of the last class, on the last day of middle school, eighth grade, right when the bell rang, and it would be all over.

Or, better than that, I would've gone backward in time to when I was in fourth grade, when Mrs. Pippin was my teacher. She was The Greatest Teacher of All Time. Maybe I could have stayed there. That was the best year ever, except for Tanner Gantt. If they had real time machines, I bet nobody would live in the present.

○ ○ ○

After Choir class ended, I just wanted to get home as fast as I could and convince my parents to move to a different city, so I could go to a different school. Maybe I could go to Kennedy Middle School? Tanner Gantt wouldn't be there. I could start all over.

That didn't happen.

I had to go to my locker first to get some books for homework. I twisted the dial on the lock. 54-72-76.

The locker didn't open.

What was the combination? I tried 74-54-76. It didn't work. I'd forgotten the combination. And I hadn't written it down on the bottom of my shoe in the morning because I got distracted by seeing Abel putting *HIS* junk in what should have been *MY* locker.

Now I had to find the grumpy janitor to open it. Did I really have to pay him? I was headed to the main office, to ask where the janitor would be, when I saw him. He was cleaning up a trash can that had been tipped over. I bet Tanner Gantt did it. The janitor was short and had really long hair. He looked extra grumpy. But I had to get my books.

I cleared my throat and said, "Excuse me, sir?"

"What do you want?" he grumbled as he turned around.

He looked like he wouldn't open my locker for a million dollars.

I started to speak, "Uh, I need—"

"Don't tell me you forgot your locker combination and you want me to go open it," he said. "I've had to open six lockers for six kids today! How hard is it to remember three numbers!"

Just then I saw Abel across the quad, walking to our locker. For the first time ever, I was glad to see him. I smiled at the janitor.

"No, sir, I didn't forget my combination. I just wanted to tell you that you're doing an excellent job. The school looks really clean. People don't appreciate how much hard work janitors do. You should get a raise."

The janitor looked at me with a surprised expression. Then he smiled. "Thanks, kid."

I ran over to Abel and watched him turn the dial to see what the combination was.

76-54-72.

"The first day of middle school has concluded," said Abel as he pulled out some books. "One down, a hundred seventy-nine to go."

A hundred seventy-nine more days of this? I didn't think I could do it.

Abel shook my hand again. "Have a splendid evening. I shall see you tomorrow, with a surprise."

He put his books into his briefcase and walked off. I was a little worried about what the surprise would be. I wrote the combination down on the bottom of my shoe with a pen, and then I put four books in my backpack. They didn't weigh twenty pounds each, like Emma said they would.

I didn't want to take the bus home. I knew Tanner Gantt would be on it and pretend to faint again and call me Fainty. Annie would be on the bus too, and I didn't want to see her after what happened in Choir class.

Finally, The Worst and Weirdest First Day of Middle School Ever had ended.

The Invisible Tom Plan had not worked out at all.

Now I just had to get home.

○ ○ ○

I saw Zeke standing by the bus, looking around for me. He almost saw me, but I ducked into the library. I hoped Annie wasn't in there. She *loves* libraries. There were only a few kids inside, some reading books, some doing homework at a big table, and some using the computers. I decided to stay in the library until the bus left and then walk home.

They had posters up on the wall to try and make kids want to read. The first poster had a picture of a vampire, in a black cape, reading the book *Dracula*. It said: "Reading Doesn't Suck!" The vampire had two fangs with blood on them. I hoped my two teeth didn't get as big and pointy as those.

READING DOESN'T SUCK!

The next poster said: "Real Werewolves Read!" There was a picture of a werewolf, sitting in a big chair by a fireplace, wearing a robe and slippers

REAL WEREWOLVES READ!

and glasses, having a cup of tea and reading a book called *Never Cry Wolf*. Why was he in a robe and wearing slippers? Would a werewolf really drink

tea? That poster bugged me. I looked at the picture of the wolf. For the first time I thought to myself, what if a wolf had bitten me and not a dog? Did I need *extra* rabies shots?

The last poster was of a zombie, reading a book. It said: "Want Brains? Read a Book!" The zombie was reading *Warm Bodies*. That poster didn't bug me. It gave me an idea.

I sat down at one of the computers and googled "T. E. Robbins Carnival of Oddities"—the name on the zombie trailer at the creepy gas station. I found a picture of Old Smelly Cigar Guy standing by the zombie trailer next to a sign that said: **No Pictures or Videos Allowed Inside!** Underneath the picture was a link to a video on YouTube. I clicked on it. Somebody must've snuck their phone inside the trailer to film it.

The video was dark, but you could make out the zombie dummy in his chair. He leaned forward, just like when I went in. But he didn't look like a dummy. He looked like a real person.

14.

A New Plan with a Bad Name

The whole time I walked home, I was thinking about all the weird stuff that had happened over the past two days. I decided I had to find out what was going on. I had a new plan.

I know that's a lame name, but I didn't have time to think of a better one.

When I got home, Mom

was standing right by the front door, all excited. She was holding an old cane that had an animal head on it. She sells antiques and other old stuff over the Internet that she finds in junk shops and yard sales. She stores all the things in our garage. Zeke *loves* to go in there. But it takes forever to get him out because he wants to pick up everything.

"So! How was the big day?" she asked, giving me a hug.

"Great," I lied.

I didn't want to tell her about the bad stuff that had happened at school.

"How'd you do in the rain?" she asked with a smile. "Didn't a wise woman say to take an umbrella to school?" She was just like Gram. She had her "I told you so" look.

"I was fine," I said. "Some kid let me share his umbrella."

"How nice! Is he a new friend?"

"No," I said.

After she asked me a million more questions, I went into the kitchen and grabbed five protein bars and slipped them in my backpack.

"I'm going over to Zeke's to do homework!" I yelled as I headed to the back door.

"Okay!" Mom yelled back. "Be home before it gets dark! Dinner's at six!"

"What are we having?"

"Steak!"

"Yes!" I said. "I want mine rare!"

"Rare? I thought you were a well-done guy?"

"Not anymore!" I ran out and jumped on my bike.

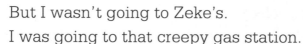

But I wasn't going to Zeke's.

I was going to that creepy gas station.

ᵒ ᵒ ᵒ

It took almost half an hour to get to the road that Gram and I had turned down. I was pedaling really fast the whole time and I never got tired. I ate the five protein bars while I rode. They must've been keeping me energized. I finally got to the turnoff. I went down the dirt road and came over the little hill.

The gas station was gone.

15.

Impossible

The station had burnt down. The main building was totally gone except for the front door. The cement bathroom walls were still there, but the roof had burnt and caved in. There was yellow police tape all over the place, and it was deserted.

It was even creepier than before.

I bet Old Smelly Cigar Guy had been smoking his cigar when someone was getting gas and the place blew up, just like Gram said. The trailer with the zombie dummy was still there, but it was all burnt black. The door was open. I went over and peeked inside.

The chair was there, but the zombie dummy was gone.

I looked down at the floor and saw footprints in the ash going from the chair out the door.

"Hey! Get out of there!"

I turned and saw a woman in an orange vest and a yellow hard hat yelling at me. I jumped back on my bike and rode away.

On the way home, I started thinking. Either somebody had taken the zombie dummy out of the trailer, probably Old Smelly Cigar Guy, or maybe . . .

I didn't want to think about the other explanation.

o o o

I got home, and Dad, Mom, and I had dinner. Emma was at Pari's house doing homework. Or at least that's what she told Mom she was doing. I told Dad about my day, in between bites of the amazingly delicious, rare piece of steak, and then Gram called. I took the phone into the living room, so Mom and Dad wouldn't hear. I told her *some* of the bad stuff that happened at school, but not the weird stuff.

"Sorry to hear that, Tommy," she said. "Well, I won't lie to you, you're going to have good days and bad days your whole life. How you deal with them is up to you. But remember, tomorrow's a new day. I think it'll be a better one. Now, I gotta scoot. Going to a meeting about that new road they want to put in by the lake— over my dead body! Call me anytime. I'm open twenty-four hours a day if you need me. Sleep tight and don't let the bedbugs bite!"

"'Night, Gram," I said, and started to hang up.

"Oh, wait!" she said. "Almost forgot. Guess what I saw sitting on the windowsill in your bedroom up here tonight?"

I wasn't sure I wanted to know.

"What?" I asked.

"A bat . . . I bet it was the same one that bit you. Probably came back for another taste."

I did a fake laugh and said, "Yeah. Uh, I gotta go do homework now, Gram. Bye."

I went upstairs to my room in a daze. I closed the door and sat down on my bed. I couldn't believe what I was thinking.

It was crazy.

It was unbelievable.

It made no sense.

It was impossible.

But . . . it explained everything.

I hadn't been bitten by a regular bat or a big dog or cut my hand on a zombie dummy's teeth.

I had been bitten by . . .

A *vampire* bat.

An actual *werewolf*.

And a *real zombie.*

I fainted for the second time that day.

16.

What Am I?

I woke up on the floor. For a second, I thought to myself, "Okay. That was just a dream. A really, really, loose, long, super-realistic dream that lasted two days."

Then I touched the bite on my neck and looked down at the bite on my ankle and the cut on my hand.

It wasn't a dream.

It was real.

It explained all the crazy stuff that had been happening.

That's why I was hungry all the time.

That's why the rare hamburger and rare steak tasted so good.

That's why I couldn't see myself in mirrors.

That's why I was so pale.

That's why my eyes were red and watery.

That's why Muffin growled at me.

That's why the sunlight coming through the window in class hurt.

That's why Ms. Heckroth's blood smelled good.

That's why the garlic on Zeke's pizza made me feel sick.

That's why I could run so fast in Phys Ed.

That's why, when the sun came out, I got sick and weak and fainted.

That's why I howled in Choir.

That's why I could pedal my bike so fast.

I was a vampire . . . a werewolf . . . and a zombie.

All three. I was a mutt. Like Muffin.

So what exactly was I?

A Vam-Wolf-Zom?

I did not have a *What If I Turn into a Vampire-Werewolf-Zombie Plan.*

o o o

It was official. I had had the worst luck of any

eleven-year-old kid in the history of eleven-year-old kids. There was only one thing I could do.

I called Zeke and told him *everything*.

There was a long pause and then he said, "EXCELLENT!"

He totally believed me right away. I knew he would.

"T-Man, I am on my way! See you in six minutes!"

Six minutes later I heard the doorbell ring. I could smell Zeke as soon as Mom opened the door. He'd had tacos for dinner. I had explained on the phone to Zeke that I'd told my mom we had already studied that day at his house, because I needed an excuse to go to the gas station. Zeke kind of got mad that I went to the gas station without him, but he never stays mad for long.

I heard him downstairs saying, "Hi, Mrs. Marks! Tom and I are gonna study some more. We're going to get straight A's in all our classes this year!"

Zeke is so bad at making stuff up. Now Mom would expect me to get straight A's.

I heard Zeke running up the stairs and down the hall. He opened my door and started to come in . . . and then he stopped in the doorway and hesitated.

"What are you doing?" I said. "Get in here and lock the door!"

He looked a little worried. "Are you gonna . . . bite me?"

"No!"

"You sure?"

"Yes!"

He still didn't come in. "Are you gonna try to suck my blood?"

"No! Gross! That's disgusting! Get in here!"

Zeke stayed in the doorway. "Are you gonna try to eat me?"

"NO!"

He shrugged. "Just asking."

Zeke came in and closed the door. I'd never seen him so excited. He was practically dancing.

"Calm down," I said in a serious voice. "Okay, Zeke. Listen to me. The most important thing: You cannot tell ANYBODY about this. You've got to swear."

Zeke raised his hand and said, "I solemnly, mega-promise-swear, that I will not tell *anyone*— even if they torture me—that my best friend, Tom Marks, also known as T-Man, is a vampire . . . and a werewolf . . . and a zombie!"

Zeke started dancing around the room again. "T-Man, this is the most awesomely excellent thing ever! This is so cool!"

"Are you crazy?" I said. "This is *horrible*! This is *awful*! This is the worst thing *ever*!"

Zeke looked at me, confused. "It is?"

"Yes! I don't want to be a vampire and a werewolf and a zombie!"

"You don't? I would LOVE to be a vampire and a werewolf and— Hey! Can I call you VWZ-Man now?"

"No!"

I could tell he was disappointed. But he always bounces back fast.

"T-Man! I almost forgot!" Zeke reached into his pocket and pulled out a piece of paper and handed it to me. "T-Man, you gotta remember some important stuff. I made a list on the way over. Keep it in your pocket at *all* times."

I looked at the list.

1. STAY OUT OF THE SUN!

2. DON'T LET ANYBODY STAB YOU IN THE HEART WITH A WOODEN STAKE.

3. DON'T LET ANYBODY SHOOT YOU WITH A SILVER BULLET.

4. DON'T LET ANYBODY CHOP OFF YOUR HEAD.

5. DON'T LET ANYBODY STICK SOMETHING SHARP INTO YOUR BRAIN.

"Uh, thanks, Zeke," I said, and put the list in my pocket. "What am I gonna do now?"

Zeke raised his right arm and pointed his finger in the air. "To the Internet!"

17.

Werewolf Perks

There were a million websites about vampires and werewolves and zombies. Zeke was sitting at my computer, scrolling through a list of them. He loves scary movies even more than my gram, and he knows a lot about monsters. I was pacing back and forth.

"Can I change back?" I asked. "Is there like a cure? Or a ritual you can do? Or a potion you can drink?"

Zeke shook his head. "Nope. Once you turn, you stay that way."

"Great," I groaned.

Zeke turned around in the chair to face me. "Wait, T-Man. Think of all the cool stuff you can do now!"

"Like what? Drink blood? Howl at the moon? Eat people?"

"You've got awesome powers—well, zombies don't have any powers, except it's way hard to kill them."

Zeke turned back to the computer and started reading out loud:

"'Werewolves possess great speed. They can travel long distances without tiring. Some can reach speeds of up to sixty miles per hour.'" He turned around and looked at me. "T-Man! You gotta go out for the track team!"

"You're forgetting about the sun," I reminded him. "I could only run inside or at night."

"Oh, yeah," he said, all disappointed. "Wait! That'll be your cool thing! You'll be called . . . Night Runner Guy!"

Zeke doesn't come up with very good names for things. He went back to the computer and read: "'Werewolves are up to five times stronger than humans.' T-Man, pick up your bed!"

"There's no way I can pick up my bed."

"I bet you can!"

I bent down
and reached under
my bed. I lifted it
up, over my head,
as easy as if it were
a pillow.

"Excellent!"

There was a knock
on the door.

"Hey, guys!" said Mom
through the door.
"How's it going?"

I froze.

"Uh . . . great, Mom," I said, still holding the bed
up. I looked over at the door handle. Zeke *hadn't*
locked it.

"What are you two studying?" she asked.

"Werewolves," said Zeke.

I wanted to kill him.

"Werewolves?" she asked, suspicious.

"Yeah!" said Zeke. "We're doing a report on
werewolves. The history, the legends. Hey, Mrs.
Marks, did you know a werewolf can run sixty
miles an hour and—"

I looked at Zeke and whispered, "Shut! Up!"

"What class is this for?" Mom asked.

"English?" said Zeke.

I thought Mom was going to open the door any second.

"We better get back to studying," I said.

"Okay," said Mom.

We heard her walk away down the hall.

I put my bed down and glared at Zeke. "We're studying *werewolves?!*"

He shrugged. "It was the first thing I could think of. Okay, I got an awesome idea. Since you're superstrong now, you can beat up Tanner Gantt!"

That was an interesting idea. I hadn't thought about that. He totally deserved it. But I'd never beaten up anybody in my life. What was that like?

Zeke kept reading off the computer. "'Werewolves also possess a super sense of smell.'"

"I know," I said. "I've been smelling things all day. Hey! How come I haven't turned into a werewolf? How come I'm not hairy everywhere?"

Zeke made his "I'm thinking" face. It's exactly the same as his "I'm totally confused" face, so you never know what he's going to say. "Maybe because you're only one-third werewolf and one-third vampire and one-third zombie? And it's not a full moon tonight?"

"Wait a minute," I said. "It wasn't a full moon two nights ago when I got bitten by that werewolf."

Zeke read on. "'Some werewolves are known

as shape-shifters and can change into a wolf at any time, others change only when the full moon appears, and a few rare species are permanently wolves.'"

I was glad I wasn't a permanent wolf.

"Werewolves have night vision!" shouted Zeke as he jumped up from the computer and ran over to the window to pull open the shutters. "Try it!"

I looked out my window at the street. It was nighttime, and I could see the houses clearly, but it was all black-and-white. It was like when people use night-vision goggles.

I saw one of our neighbors, Professor Beiersdorfer, who lives right across the street. He was in his backyard, digging a hole. He's an old, retired scientist. I didn't know why he was digging a hole at night in his backyard, but he does weird stuff like that.

I saw Mrs. Korkis, our next-door neighbor. She was walking her dog and it was pooping. It's a big, giant police dog, so it was a big, giant poop that was really gross and disgusting.

So far this night vision wasn't so great.

I looked down the street—where it was dark because one of the streetlights was out—and I could see two teenagers, inside a parked car, kissing. They broke apart to breathe.

The girl was Emma.

I did *not* want to see that. She was kissing this guy named Lucas Barrington, which was completely insane. Lucas used to mow our lawn when they were in middle school. He was this tall, skinny guy with red hair, and he always wore an orange T-shirt and a green hat. Emma called him Carrot Boy.

She used to watch him, from our living room window, and say, "Okay, that is, like, the oddest-looking person I have ever seen. He looks like a carrot. Seriously. And he's so skinny, and look at his hair. It is so messy and curly and gross."

I had to agree with her, for once. Lucas was never going to be a movie star. But, I guess Emma had changed her mind.

"What do you see?" asked Zeke, who was standing right next to me.

"You're not gonna believe it. Emma is in a car kissing Lucas Barrington."

"What?! No way!" Zeke got upset. He likes Emma. He thinks she's pretty. He's crazy.

Lucas rolled down the car window because the windows were fogging up. I opened my window to see if I could hear what they were saying, the same way I had heard those girls in the back row of History class talking about me. I leaned out the window and I could totally hear them talking.

"I really like you, Emma."

"I really like you, Lucas."

"I didn't think you liked me."

"I didn't think you liked me, either."

"I like your hair. It's so black."

"I like yours. It's so curly."

"I like your eyes."

"I like your eyes too."

"You've got an awesome smile."

"I had braces."

"Me too."

"Braces suck."

"Yeah."

This was The Most Boring Conversation of All Time.

"What are they saying?" asked Zeke.

"Lame stuff," I said, closing the window. "So, what can vampires do?"

"'*Vampires don't grow old*,'" said Zeke, back at the computer.

"What?" I panicked. "I'm always going to be eleven? My *whole* life? What—I'll never get a driver's license!"

Zeke sadly nodded. "And you won't be able to go to an R-rated movie or skydive or buy fireworks or a lottery ticket or gamble or vote or get a tattoo or a piercing."

Sometimes the stuff that Zeke knows is surprising.

"I don't want to be a kid forever!" I said.

"My dad says he wishes he could've been a kid forever," said Zeke.

I nodded. "Yeah, adults *always* say that. But that's because they forget how hard it is to be a kid."

I sat down on the edge of my bed. Annie would never be my girlfriend if I stayed eleven forever. That meant *no* mansion. *No* private island. And nobody to throw food at Tanner Gantt.

"Wait a minute," said Zeke. "You'll still turn eighteen and get older."

"I will?"

"Definitely," said Zeke.

That was good news. I felt a lot better.

But then Zeke went on. "You just won't *look* old. You'll always look eleven."

"What?! I don't want to look eleven forever!" Then I realized it didn't matter what I looked like or how old I was. Annie would never go on a date or marry or even hang out with a vampire-werewolf-zombie. I lay back on my bed and stared at the ceiling.

My life sucked.

Zeke kept reading off the computer. "'Some vampires live to be three or four hundred years old.' T-Man! Think how many birthday gifts and Christmas presents you'll get!"

I didn't care.

"Okay. Seriously," said Zeke, "you do have one problem."

"*One* problem? I've got a million problems!"

"I'm talking about blood. Have you thought about how you're going to get blood?"

"No," I said. "I figured out I was a vampire like half an hour ago!"

"Maybe they sell blood on Amazon?"

Zeke is crazy.

"They don't sell blood on Amazon!" I said.

Zeke started typing. "They sell *everything*! My dad says you can get *anything* on Amazon. He once bought two hissing cockroaches. Look! They have it! Bucket of Blood! It's only twenty dollars! See! I was right!"

I looked at the screen and saw a picture of a big, red plastic bucket of blood.

"Zeke, that's *fake* blood for a show or for Halloween. Wait, why did your dad buy hissing cockroaches?"

Zeke jumped out of the chair and looked at me like he had just won the lottery. "T-Man, we gotta go up on your roof!"

"Why?" I asked, a little worried.

"Vampires can shape-shift! We gotta see if you can turn into a bat . . . and fly!"

18.

Creaky Floors

We had to get on the roof without my parents knowing. We were NEVER supposed to go up on our roof because it was "too dangerous." My dad fell off a roof when he was seven years old and broke his leg. Or was it his arm? Or his hand? He broke *something*. So, he was always telling us, "Do not *think* about going up on the roof or you will be in big trouble!"

Zeke and I tiptoed down the hallway and went in a closet.

"I *love* to go into closets," whispered Zeke.

We closed the door behind us quietly, and climbed the steep, narrow staircase that goes up to our attic. Our attic is filled with a lot of junk my parents won't throw away, like old furniture, clothes nobody wears anymore, a drum set my dad used to play, and a million boxes.

Zeke and I carefully walked across the wooden floor. My parents' bedroom was *right* underneath us. I could hear them watching TV. It seemed like every step we took made a creaking noise. If my parents heard us, we'd have to invent a really good reason for being up there.

We were almost to the window that we could open and crawl out onto the roof, when Zeke knocked over a box, because he was looking at all the junk. He gets distracted easily.

The box landed with a big *thud*, and we both froze.

I could hear Mom's and Dad's muffled voices through the floor.

"What was that?" said Dad, all suspicious.

"Nothing," said Mom. "Shh. I'm trying to watch this show."

"It sounded like somebody's up in the attic."

"Shhh!"

"Are Tom and Zeke up in the attic?"

"No. They're in Tom's room studying about werewolves."

"Werewolves?" said my dad, excited. "I *love* werewolves. Should I go in and help them?"

"No!"

Mom turned up the volume on the TV.

I bent down to put the box back and then I dragged Zeke over to the window I pushed it open and we crawled out onto the roof.

"T-Man!" he whispered. "There's your helicopter!"

It was a remote-controlled helicopter that I got last Christmas. Emma had landed it on the roof (on purpose!), and Dad wouldn't get it for me because of his *No One Must Ever Go on the Roof Rule*. Zeke picked it up, but I made him leave it there, because if Dad saw it in my room he'd know we'd been on the roof.

We stood up and looked around. There were a lot of stars in the sky and an almost full moon. With my night vision I could see the park a block away. Zeke and I used to go there when we were little. They had swings and slides and a pirate ship you could climb on. The park looked empty, but then I saw somebody on the swings. It was Tanner Gantt. He was sitting on a swing, but he wasn't swinging. He was just sitting there, all by himself. I wondered what he was doing. I bet he was planning stuff to do to kids the next day. I wondered if he made lists too.

Tanner Gantt's List of Things to Do to Kids

1. Push Tommy Farts into a trash can.
2. Make fun of Annie Barstow's glasses.
3. Tease Abel about his stupid suits.
4. Tell all the new kids that Dog Hots loves to be called Dog Hots.
5. Throw a rotten banana at a random kid.
6. Make up new nickname for Tommy Farts.

7. Think of a good gang name.
8. Start gang.
9. Stuff Farts or Zimmerman or Abel into their locker.
10. Hide some kid's jock strap.

I looked down at our driveway. It was a *long* way down. I would definitely not want to fall off. I could see how my dad broke whatever it was he broke when he fell off his roof.

Zeke wetted the end of his finger in his mouth, then held it up. "No wind. Clear sky. Perfect flight conditions." He turned to me. "Okay, T-Man . . . turn into a bat!"

I crossed my arms and stared at him. "How?"

"Close your eyes . . . and then say, 'I am a bat.'"

That sounded like the *dumbest* idea ever. But sometimes Zeke has dumb ideas and they actually work, so I decided to try it. I closed my eyes. I took a deep breath and then let it out. "I am a— Hey, wait a minute."

"What's the matter?" said Zeke.

"What if I turn into a bat and then I can't turn back into me?"

"Don't worry. That never happens."

"How do you know?"

"Well . . ." he said. "I've never *seen* it happen in a movie or on TV or in a book."

"But that doesn't mean it can't happen!"

"T-Man, you're not going to be a bat forever!"

"That's easy for you to say. You're not turning into a bat."

Zeke sighed. "Okay, okay. *If* you turn into a bat and you can't turn back, I promise I'll keep you as my pet."

"WHAT?! I don't want to be your pet bat!"

Zeke got all offended. "Why not? I'd treat you nice. I'd feed you and clean your cage every day."

"You'd put me in a *cage*?!"

"Well, yeah. My mom wouldn't let me have a bat in the house. But I'd let you out at night to fly around the neighborhood."

"Zeke, there is *no way* I am going to be your pet bat!"

That's when we heard a voice coming from below us, in the front yard.

"What are you two losers doing up there?"

19.

Blackmail

We looked down, and there was Emma, standing in the driveway, looking up at us.

"We're doing a report for Science class," I said quickly, so Zeke wouldn't say something ridiculous.

"A report about *what*?" said Emma suspiciously.

"Roofs," said Zeke.

ZEKE IS THE WORST LIAR IN THE WORLD!

"It's not about

roofs!" I said, giving Zeke a look. "It's a report about . . . stars."

Emma crossed her arms and smirked. "Yeah, right. I'm telling Dad you're on the roof."

"No! Don't!" I yelled. "Come on, Emma, why do you even care if we're up here?"

Emma did a voice like she was talking to a two-year-old kid. "*Because* if you fall and break your neck, you'll go to the hospital. Then, Mom and Dad will force me to go visit you every day. Then, I'll have to sit by your bed and talk to you, and that would be the most boring thing in the world!"

"Emma, *please* don't tell Dad we're on the roof," I pleaded.

She started walking toward the front door. "Dad!"

It was blackmail time. She gave me no choice.

I yelled down at her, "If you do it, I'll tell them you were making out with Lucas Barrington."

Emma froze. She jerked her head up at me. She looked like she was going to have a heart attack. It was pretty funny.

"I wasn't . . . How'd you . . . Where were—?" She was freaking out. "Were you spying on me, you little creeps?"

"I wasn't spying on you, Emma," said Zeke,

holding up his hand like he was swearing to something. "I promise!"

I shrugged and said, "I was just looking down the street and I saw what I saw."

Emma looked back down the street, where Lucas's car had been parked, and then turned back to me. "How'd you see us that far away?"

Before I could say anything, Zeke opened his big, fat mouth, "Because he's—"

I cut him off. "Because . . . the moonlight—and you can see stuff really clear from up here."

Emma had never been up on the roof, so I hoped she would believe me.

"Okay!" she said. "Go ahead and break your neck. But I'm not visiting you at the hospital!"

She went in the house and slammed the front door.

I heard Dad yell from the bedroom, "Don't slam the door!"

Emma is The Queen of Door Slammers.

Zeke turned to me, all sad. "Do you think Emma's going to marry Lucas Barrington?"

I didn't want to stand up on the roof and talk about Emma and Lucas. I wanted to try to turn into a bat and fly.

"No, Zeke!" I said. "She's going to marry you."

I was totally making a joke, but Zeke thought I was being serious. He does that a lot.

"Excellent!" he said, excited.

"Okay, okay, how do I turn into a bat?"

"Uh . . . I don't know. Just say 'I am a bat.'"

I said, "I am . . . a bat."

I waited a little bit.

I wasn't a bat.

"Maybe you should whisper it?" suggested Zeke.

"Why?"

"It'll sound cooler."

I whispered, "I am a bat."

It didn't sound cooler to me.

Nothing happened.

"Maybe you should close your eyes," said Zeke, "and concentrate on picturing yourself as a bat."

I closed my eyes. For some reason I pictured myself with a tiny bat head with big, buggy eyes on top of a regular-sized human torso and legs, with two giant bat wings instead of arms. It was creepy looking.

And it didn't work.

I was still just a kid standing on a roof.

I think Zeke was more disappointed than I was. "Aw, man! I really wanted to see you fly."

"Let's go back inside before my parents catch us," I said.

We turned around to head back inside, and that's when I tripped on the stupid helicopter (that Emma flew up there on purpose) and fell off the roof.

20.

Landing

I rolled down the roof and over the edge. It's crazy what you can think about in a few seconds. I wondered what I was going to break:

My arms?

My legs?

My feet?

My back?

My neck?

All of the above?

I also thought, as I was falling, that this would be a *great* time to turn into a bat and fly. That way

I wouldn't smash into the brick walkway and break anything.

I didn't turn into a bat.

But I didn't break anything either.

I landed on my feet, like a cat, and it didn't hurt. I looked up at Zeke, who was standing at the edge of the roof, grinning.

"Sweet landing, T-Man!"

The front door opened, and there was Dad. "What are you doing out here, Tom? I thought you were studying werewolves up in your room."

"I . . . I . . . I'm doing homework now for Science class," I said. "We're studying the stars."

"Really?" said Dad, coming out onto the walkway and looking up, right where Zeke was standing on the roof.

I grabbed Dad's arm and turned him away in the opposite direction and pointed up at the sky.

"What's that star, Dad?"

"Well, actually that's not a star, that's a planet, that's Mercury. Stars twinkle, planets have a steady light." He looked around. "Where's Zeke? He should be hearing this."

"He's . . . in the bathroom."

Zeke always went to the bathroom at least three times when he was at my house. He has The World's Smallest Bladder.

I had to stand outside *forever* with my dad and talk about stars and planets. Zeke quietly crawled across the roof, through the attic window, and back into the house. He finally came out the front door. Dad talked some more about stars until Zeke's mom called and he had to go home.

"See you tomorrow, Zeke," I said.

"See you on the bus, T-Man."

"Hey, Tom," said Dad, "we should do this again tomorrow night. There's going to be a full moon."

21.

Nightmare

That night I had a bizarre dream. The carnival trailer from the gas station was parked in front of my house. There was a big sign on it that said:

SEE THE VAM WOLF ZOM!
3 MONSTERS FOR THE PRICE OF 1!

Old Smelly Cigar Guy was standing on a box talking to a crowd of people.

"Ladies and gentlemen, step right up and see a sight that is so strange, so utterly monstrous, so horrible, that I urge any of you who are easily

frightened or upset, who have a weak heart or queasy stomach and any small children, to refrain from going inside to see the most incredible oddity on the planet! Terrifying Tom: The World's One and Only Vam-Wolf-Zom! Only five dollars! Talk to it! Ask it questions! Take a selfie! You can even poke it with a stick if you brought one! And if you didn't bring a stick, I will sell you one for only one dollar! But be warned: Don't get too close! He bites! And if he bites you . . . you will become . . . as horrible as he is!"

Then, Annie walked up with Zeke, but they were both older. They looked about twenty-five years old. But that wasn't the weirdest thing. Annie was in a long, white dress, and Zeke was wearing a tuxedo.

They paid Old Smelly Cigar Guy five dollars each and walked inside the trailer.

There I was, tied up in the chair, just like the zombie. I still looked eleven years old.

"Annie! Zeke!" I yelled. "I'm so glad to see you! Help me! Get me out of here!"

"Hi, T-Man," said Zeke. "You look excellent!"

"Why are you both so dressed up?" I asked.

Annie smiled. "Hi, Tom. Well, Zeke and I are getting married today. I'm really sorry, I can't marry a vampire-werewolf-zombie. But we wanted you to be here."

"What?!" I shouted.

Zeke said, "T-Man, will you be my best man?"

"No way!"

Then Tanner Gantt came in. He was older too. He had on a black coat with a white collar around his neck. He was the *minister* who was going to marry them! How did Tanner Gantt become a minister?!

"Zeke Zimmerman," said Tanner, in a deep voice. "Do you take the amazingly awesome, smart, cool, pretty, and funny Annie Barstow to be your lawfully wedded wife?"

"I do!" said Zeke.

"Annie Barstow, do you take Zeke Zimmerman to be your lawfully wedded husband, instead of this gross, disgusting, scary vampire-werewolf-zombie thing, that I can hardly bear to look at?"

"I do!" said Annie.

Tanner smiled. "May I have the rings, please?"

Zeke looked at me. "Give us the rings, T- Man. They're in your front pocket."

I managed to reach into the front pocket of my jeans, even though I was tied up. There were two rings! How did they get in there?

"I'm not going to give you any rings!" I said.

Tanner Gantt went to take the rings out of my hand, and I tried to bite him.

"T-Man! Don't bite the minister!" yelled Zeke.

Tanner Gantt said, "Don't worry, Zeke, I got this." He pulled a wooden stake out of his jacket, raised his arm up, and was about to stab me.

"No! Don't stab him! He's my best man!" Zeke cried.

I woke up.

It was the most bizarre dream I had ever had in my life.

But the next day was even more bizarre.

22.

Here Comes the Sun

"**G**et up, Mr. Middle School Man!" said Mom as she passed by my door.

I hoped she wasn't going to do that *every* single morning.

I made sure I ate a humongous breakfast, so I wouldn't be starving.

1. *A big bowl of cereal*
2. *Two eggs (scrambled)*
3. *Three pieces of bacon (extra crispy)*
4. *Three pancakes (with butter and syrup)*
5. *Orange juice (with no pulp)*

"I'm going to have to get another job, so I can afford to keep feeding you!" said Dad.

Nobody laughed except my mom, who was looking out the window. "I'm so glad the sun's out today, not gloomy like yesterday."

Muffin sat in the corner, as far away from me as possible, and stared at me.

"You better apologize to Muffin," said Mom. "He's still mad at you for growling at him yesterday."

I was going to remind her that Muffin growled at me *first,* but I didn't. Now I understood why Muffin had growled at me. He knew I was part werewolf.

"Sorry, Muff," I said.

Emma watched me put a bunch of protein bars in my backpack and said, "Please say you're running away from home?"

I ignored her. Sometimes that's the best thing to do.

It took so long to make my breakfast and eat it and clean everything up, that I was afraid I was going to miss the bus. I ran out of the house, forgetting something very important.

I was about halfway down the block when all of a sudden it felt like I was getting The Worst Sunburn in the World. Every single part of my body that was exposed to the sun felt like it was burning up. My arms hurt, my hands hurt, my face hurt, my eyes hurt, my ears hurt, even my hair hurt. That's when I remembered I was one-third vampire and the sun was *not* my friend. I looked down at my arms. They were *smoking.*

"OWWWWWW!" I cried.

It was ten times worse than when I was running track because the sun had already been out a while, and it was super bright.

I ran back to the house as fast as I could. As soon as I got inside I felt better. I caught my breath and then I ran up the stairs. Emma was coming down, talking on her phone. "Pari, you are *not* going to believe what happened

with you-know-who last night!" I sort of bumped into Emma, and she sort of fell down, and I sort of stepped on her ankle.

"You stupid dork!" she yelled. "You almost killed me!"

"Emma! Do not call your brother a 'stupid dork'!" yelled Mom from the kitchen.

"But he is a stupid dork! I think he just broke my ankle! I can't walk! Call nine-one-one!"

She is so dramatic.

I needed major sun protection and I was in a hurry.

I opened my closet and grabbed the first hat I saw. It was bright green and had a Tyrannosaurus rex with short, red punk hair and sunglasses playing a guitar. It said: **DINOSAURS ROCK!** I got it at this place called Dino World when I was seven years old and I thought it was the coolest hat I'd ever seen in my life. I would *never* wear it now, but it was the only one I could find, and I was already late.

I was hoping that people would think I was being cool and funny because I was wearing a hat that was for little kids. Last year, Jason Gruber wore a *Dora the Explorer* hat, and everybody thought he was totally cool and funny. But Jason can wear *anything,* and look cool. I don't know how he does it.

You can wear hats to school as long as you take them off in class and they don't have offensive things written on them. Last year, Tanner Gantt wore a hat that said **SCHOOL SUCKS!** He got in serious trouble.

Next, I grabbed a pair of sunglasses that I had worn in a third-grade talent show. Zeke and I did an act where we were supposed to be The Elvis Presley Twins. We lip-synched to one of his songs called "Hound Dog." There were fourteen acts in the show. We won *fourteenth* place. That's because Zeke never learned the words to the song. He also didn't really know who Elvis Presley was, so that didn't help either. Annie won first place, and she deserved it, because she actually sang a song and played guitar and had talent.

I yanked off my T-shirt and put on a long-sleeve, button-up one that Mom forces me to wear when I have to dress up and "look nice." I put sunscreen all over my face, neck, ears, and hands, which was hard because . . . I COULDN'T SEE MY REFLECTION IN THE MIRROR!

Since I was going to have to do this stuff every single day I would probably have to get up earlier. If I didn't do this stuff, I would end up a big pile of ashes on the sidewalk.

I decided that if I *ever* saw that stupid vampire bat, I was going to do something really terrible to it. I didn't know what, but I enjoyed thinking about the possibilities.

∘ ∘ ∘

When I ran out of the house, Emma was walking to Pari's car.

"I thought you broke your ankle?" I said.

"It got better," she said as she noticed what I was wearing. "Cool hat. And I *love* the sunglasses. Wow. I didn't know it was Be a Mime Day."

"It's sunscreen!"

"Oh yeah? Are you taking a field trip to the sun?"

I got a little worried. "Did I put too much on?"

Emma smiled. "No. Not at all."

I knew that meant I had put way too much on. I ran to the bus stop, hoping the sunscreen would eventually get absorbed into my skin and I wouldn't look like a mime or a clown. When I finally got to the bus stop, there was nobody there.

I'd missed the bus.

23.

Speedster

I was going to get marked tardy.

One tardy gets you a warning.

Two tardies means you have to go to Silent Lunch Detention. You can't talk the whole time and you have to sit at a special table, facing the wall, with a lot of kids you probably don't want to have lunch with.

Three tardies means you have to do "campus beautification," which is just a fancy word for picking up trash. You're basically doing the janitor's job, but not getting paid for it.

Four tardies means one-hour detention after school—with people like Tanner Gantt.

Five tardies means Saturday school—with people like Tanner Gantt and maybe even worse.

 ° ° °

I started to run. Maybe I could get to the next bus stop before the bus did. I took a shortcut through an alley, and three different dogs barked at me.

I came out of the alley and saw the bus drive by. I ran down the sidewalk, toward the bus stop. I looked over and noticed that I was *passing* the bus. I got to the stop just as the bus pulled up.

Bus Lady opened the door and said, "Man, you got some serious speed, kid! I'm going to call you The Speedster!"

I guess there are worse nicknames than that.

Now that I knew the cross on her necklace would

make me feel sick—because I was a vampire—I just smiled and walked by.

I went down the aisle toward Zeke, who was sitting in the back of the bus. Some of the kids gave me weird looks and said stuff as I walked by.

"Nice sunglasses, Mr. Cool!"

"Can I have your autograph, please?"

"You 'spose to be a clown?"

"It's not Halloween, dork!"

"Wow! Do dinosaurs really rock?"

"That is one lame hat, wimp!"

I was definitely not Jason Gruber.

○ ○ ○

At least Tanner Gantt wasn't on the bus. That was good news. He'd probably ditched school, or hopefully he had gotten arrested for robbing a bank or something.

Annie was sitting next to Capri, the girl from my Art class. They were talking, so I just nodded at Annie as I walked by. Capri gave me a strange look, but so did practically everybody else on the bus. I sat down next to Zeke in the back.

"Excellent hat!" he said. He wasn't being sarcastic. Zeke loved to go to Dino World. "I used to have a hat like that, but my old dog, Tucker, ate it, then he puked it up, it was gross, but I didn't want to throw it away, so I washed it five times.

But it still smelled like dog puke, so I had to throw
it away. Hey. Why is your face so white?"

"Sunscreen," I said. "Shhh!"

Annie and Capri were talking to each other and
I wanted to hear what they were saying. Most of
the kids on the bus were talking, so it was pretty
noisy. But if I turned one of my ears directly toward
them, I could hear perfectly.

"Do you know Tom Marks?" Capri asked Annie.

"Yeah. We went to elementary school together."

"He's in my Art class. He's a *terrible* artist. I
mean, he is like the *worst* artist I have ever seen in
my life. Why is he taking Art class? He can't draw
at all."

"Maybe that's why he's taking Art class, so he can learn how," said Annie.

This obviously hadn't occurred to Capri. She thought about it for a moment and then said, "What is up with that hat he's wearing and the sunglasses?"

Annie shrugged.

Capri turned around and looked right at me. I quickly pretended to be talking to Zeke. I didn't say anything to him, so I could hear what Annie was saying. I just opened and closed my mouth. Zeke seemed worried.

"T-Man! Your voice is *gone!*"

"Shhh!"

Capri turned back to Annie and said, "He's got cute ears. Kind of like an elf."

I really hoped she wasn't going to start calling me Elfy.

24.

Abel's Surprise

We finally got to school. I went to my locker and there was Abel, in a different suit. This one had a little gold chain coming out the pocket, attached to one of the buttons.

"Greetings, Mr. Marks!" he said. "Wearing sunscreen, I see. Intelligent decision. Ultraviolet rays can be deadly. I apply a sunscreen with a protection factor of eighty on a daily basis."

I could have guessed that Abel wore sunscreen.

He pointed at my sunglasses. "I believe those are the same sunglasses you wore in the Elvis Presley

act that you performed with your colleague Zeke at the talent show in third grade?"

Abel had done a ventriloquist act that year, with a dummy he dressed up to look exactly like him. A lot of kids didn't get the jokes, but I thought it was pretty funny and he came in second place, after Annie.

Abel looked up at my hat. "And a Dino World chapeau. I approve!"

I knew that *chapeau* was French for "hat." My mom had tried to get our whole family to learn how to speak French one summer at the library. We lasted one day.

Well, so far, two people liked my hat. Zeke and Abel.

Abel went on: "And I couldn't help noticing that the Tyrannosaurus rex is playing a Gibson Sunburst Les Paul guitar. That is *precisely* the same type of guitar that I play."

Abel played guitar? I always thought he'd be the type to play violin or the harp.

He pointed to our open locker. "Do you approve?"
I turned and looked.

There was wallpaper on the back of the door, a mirror and a cup filled with pens and pencils, and a little dry-erase board. He had already written something on it:

"Each day we can take turns writing inspirational sayings," said Abel. "I took the liberty of using the bottom shelf for my books, since I am of a slightly shorter stature than you. You may have the higher shelf. I hope you don't mind. I have arranged my books sequentially, from first period to sixth. I have also stocked our locker with a flashlight, first aid kit, and healthy snacks."

How early had he gotten to school to do all this? I had to say *something* to him about the locker, since he had done a lot of work. "Uh, looks good, Abel."

I wondered what he'd say if he knew he was sharing a locker with a vampire-werewolf-zombie. He'd probably say something like, "How absolutely fascinating!"

I put my books on the top shelf and said, "I've got to get to class."

Abel reached for the gold chain on his vest and pulled out a pocket watch. "Indeed. Time waits for no man. Be seeing you!"

I walked away and went around the corner and into the hallway.

"Good morning, Fainty!"

25.

Look into My Eyes

Unfortunately, Tanner Gantt *hadn't* ditched school or been arrested.

He saw my hat and laughed. "Awwww. Do you wuv dinosaurs, widdle baby Fainty? What's with the sunglasses? You trying to look cool? Trust me, Fainty, you will *never* be cool." He leaned closer. "*What* is on your face? Are you wearing makeup?"

"It's sunscreen," I said, and started to walk away.

Tanner Gantt put his arm around my shoulder, like we were friends. His big right arm felt really

heavy. I knew that any second, he was probably going to put me in a headlock.

I wondered what would happen if he knew that I could bite his neck, or rip his throat out, or claw at his heart, or eat his brains.

Would he scream?

Would he cry?

Would he pee in his pants?

Would he faint?

I would *love* to see Tanner Gantt faint. But I couldn't do any of those things to him.

First, everyone would know my secret.

Second, I would get arrested and go to prison.

Third—I didn't get to third because Tanner Gantt said, "Hey, listen, Fainty, I forgot to give you something yesterday."

"What?" I said with a sigh, knowing *exactly* what was going to happen.

"A mega-wedgie!" he shouted, pulling me under a stairway, where nobody could see us.

Now what usually happened next was this: Tanner Gantt would grab the top of your underwear and yank it up and lift you up off the ground. He was an expert at wedgies. He could teach a class called How to Give the Perfect Wedgie. He'd been giving wedgies since kindergarten and had perfected his technique. He moved really fast. You didn't even see it happen. But you felt it. And it didn't feel good.

But this time something different happened. Something that had *never* happened in the history of Tanner Gantt giving wedgies. I moved faster than he did. I grabbed both his wrists and stopped him. He tried to move his arms, but he couldn't. He looked at me half-mad and half-confused. "What are you doing?!"

To be honest, I didn't know what I was doing. It just happened.

"No more wedgies," I said quietly.

"Yeah, right!" he said, struggling to get out of my grip. "When I figure out how to get out of this stupid hold, I'm gonna throw you in that trash can!" He jerked his head toward a trash can out in the hallway.

"No, you're not," I said.

That's when I got an idea for a new plan.

The Hypnotize Tanner Gantt Plan.

o o o

Zeke had reminded me the night before that vampires can hypnotize people. They can stare into somebody's eyes and speak in a weird voice, and then they tell the person what to do and the person does it. Dracula had done it in that old movie Gram and I watched at her house.

I stared at Tanner Gantt and talked slowly, in a deep voice. "*Look* . . . into . . . my . . . eyes."

"I can't see your eyes, idiot! You're wearing sunglasses."

I had forgotten that very important fact. I couldn't let go of his wrists, so I shook my head a few times and my sunglasses fell off. We were inside, so the sun couldn't hurt my eyes.

I stared at him as hard as I could.

He laughed. "Are you trying to look tough, Fainty?"

"*Look* into my eyes," I said in my deep vampire voice.

"Why are you talking like that?" he sneered.

"*Look* into my *eyes*," I repeated.

"I don't want to look into your stupid eyes!"

The Hypnotize Tanner Gantt Plan wasn't working. It had turned into *The World's Stupidest Plan*. But for some reason I didn't stop. "Are you *afraid* to look into my eyes?"

"Afraid? Of *you*? No frickin' way!"

"Then *look* into my eyes!"

Finally, he looked right into my eyes. I stopped using the vampire voice, because it did sound kind of stupid. I spoke slowly and quietly in my normal voice. "From now on you will be nice to people. You will not tease them, or make fun of them, or call them names, or throw them in trash cans."

Tanner Gantt's eyes kind of glazed over. He didn't say anything. His mouth slowly opened a little. He spoke in a soft voice. "Yes, Tom . . . I will do everything you say."

It was working!

I was hypnotizing him!

No more bullying!

No more wedgies!

No more being tossed in trash cans!

I let go of his wrists.

That was a big mistake.

Tanner Gantt was *pretending* to be hypnotized.

∘ ∘ ∘

Before I knew what was happening, he had dragged me out from under the stairway and thrown me in the nearest trash can. It was full of yesterday's leftover lunches. You'd think the grumpy janitor would empty the trash cans out each night.

I was sitting on old apple cores, half-eaten peanut butter sandwiches, potato chip crumbs, bits of sticky fruit rolls, and pieces of soggy hamburger buns.

This was the first time I'd been thrown in a trash

can by Tanner Gantt. Somehow, by being careful, I had avoided it. But I guess in the end it had to happen to everybody.

He was laughing like this was the funniest thing in the history of the world, even though he'd done it a million times to a million kids.

"What is going on here?" said a grown-up voice. I turned my head and saw Ms. Heckroth, my strict Math teacher, standing there, looking at me. I didn't know whether I should stay in the trash can or get out. I decided to stay.

"You're one of my students, aren't you?" she said. "What is your name?"

"Tom Marks," I said, noticing a Band-Aid on the finger that she had cut yesterday.

"Who put you in that trash can, Mr. Marks?"

That was a complicated question to answer. I had two choices:

Choice #1: *I could not tell on Tanner Gantt, and he would continue to torture me forever.*
Choice #2: *I could tell on Tanner Gantt, and he would get in trouble, and then he would still torture me forever.*

Tanner Gantt gave me a look that basically said: "If you tell her I did it, you will die a slow, horrible, painful death."

This confirmed what I thought would happen if I went with Choice #2, so I went with Choice #1.

"I fell in, Ms. Heckroth," I said.

"You *fell* in?" she said, raising her eyebrow.

It sounded like she didn't believe me, so I added some details. "I was looking for my book *White Fang*, which I accidentally dropped in there."

I hoped she didn't see my copy of *White Fang* sticking out of my backpack. Out of the corner of my eye I could see Tanner Gantt slowly starting to sneak away.

"Stop right there," said Ms. Heckroth. "What is your name, young man?"

Tanner Gantt did his big, fake smile and said, "Abel Sherrill."

He was *good* at this.

"What happened, Mr. Sherrill?" she asked.

"Well, Tom was just walking down the hall, minding his own business, and this mean little kid, named Zeke Zimmerman, came up and threw him in the trash can for no reason at all and then he ran away, before I could stop him."

Tanner Gantt was *very* good at this.

Ms. Heckroth nodded. "How interesting."

"I've got to get to class now," he said as he walked away.

"One minute!" she said. "Could you please spell your last name for me, Mr. Sherrill?"

"What?" said Tanner Gantt. He did not see that coming.

"*Spell* your last name," said Ms. Heckroth. "You do know how to spell your last name, don't you?"

"Yeah . . . uh . . . S-H-A-R . . . E?" He was starting to sweat. "R-U-L . . . Can I start over?"

"No, you can't," snapped Ms. Heckroth. "Abel Sherrill is one of my students. What is your name?"

For a second, I thought to myself, it was only the second day of school, how did she know who Abel Sherrill was? Then I realized. Duh. How many kids wore a three-piece suit to school and carried a briefcase and umbrella?

"Tanner Gantt," he mumbled.

"Speak up."

"TANNER GANTT!"

"Well, Mr. Gantt, first you are going to help Mr. Marks out of the trash can that you threw him into."

"I didn't throw him in!" he protested.

"I saw you do it, Mr. Gantt."

Tanner Gantt walked over and grabbed my arm and yanked me out of the trash can. By now there was a big group of kids watching us.

"Now you will apologize to Mr. Marks," said Ms. Heckroth.

Tanner Gantt made a noise that *might* have been "Sorry."

"Enunciate, please," said Ms. Heckroth, "so Mr. Marks can understand you."

"SOR-RY!" he yelled, and started to walk away.

"Stop, Mr. Gantt. You are coming with me to the principal's office."

He spun around. "What?"

And we will be calling your parents."

All of a sudden, his face went pale and almost looked as white as mine.

In a quiet, small voice that I had never heard before, Tanner Gantt said, "Ms. Heckroth, *please* don't call my parents."

"We will discuss that with Principal Gonzales." She turned and walked toward the office. Tanner Gantt followed behind her, walking slowly, with his head down.

I was wiping some peanut butter off my pants when Zeke ran up. I told him what happened.

"You *seriously* tried to hypnotize him?" he asked.

"Yes! And it *didn't* work! You told me that vampires could hypnotize people!"

"Oh . . . yeah . . . I guess I forgot to tell you that vampires can't hypnotize someone who doesn't want to be hypnotized."

"Thanks for leaving that out," I said as I pulled a brown banana peel out of my shirt pocket.

26.

Vlad the Impaler

I got to first period, and Mr. Kessler read a chapter of *White Fang* out loud to us for a while. There's one part where some wolves eat a bunch of sled dogs and a man. That made me really hungry. Just before class ended, I heard yelling outside. I looked across the room, out the window, and saw Tanner Gantt and a woman, who must have been his mom, walking toward the parking lot.

"I had to leave work and drive all the way over here to pick you up!" she shouted. She opened the passenger door of the car and grabbed Tanner

Gantt's arm and yanked him into the front seat. "What is *wrong* with you?" She got in the driver's side of the car, and just before she slammed her door shut, I heard her say, "You stupid idiot!"

Then they drove away.

o o o

The rest of my day wasn't completely horrible. The sunscreen had absorbed into my face, so I didn't look like a mime anymore.

Mr. Prady, the Science teacher, made me, Dog Hots, and some other kid move a big bookshelf across the room. I didn't try too hard, so they wouldn't know how strong I was.

Dog Hots yelled at me, "Marks! You weakling! You're not doing anything! Push!"

I was tempted to pick up the bookshelf by myself, lift it over my head, and say, "Is this better, Dog Hots?" But I didn't.

o o o

In History class, Zeke nodded to me from two rows over and held up a note.

I shook my head. That didn't stop him. Zeke *loves* to pass notes. He usually writes things like "Meet me after school!" which is ridiculous because I *always* meet him after school. Sometimes he just draws pictures. Zeke is an even worse artist than me, so I *never* know what it is. One time he wrote a note to me and all it said was "This is a note."

Zeke passed the note to Dog Hots, who started to read it. I tried to grab it from him, but the teacher, Mrs. Troller, saw me.

"May I have that, please?" she said.

I handed the note to her and she held it up in the air. "Just so you all know, if you pass a note in my class and I catch you . . . I read it out loud."

I *hate* it when teachers read notes out loud. That should be against the law.

I had *no* idea what Zeke had written. I sunk down in my seat and prepared for the worst.

Mrs. Troller cleared her throat and read the note to the class. "'Vampires can get blood from cooking a raw piece of steak, on each side, for one minute. You squeeze the meat over a glass and blood comes out.'"

I wished I had that time machine again.

"Tom and I are writing a graphic novel about a vampire!" Zeke announced.

Mrs. Troller nodded, like teachers do. I couldn't tell if she believed him or not.

"I don't like note passing in class," she said.

I *knew* we were going to get in trouble.

"But I do like graphic novels," she added.

What?! She looked like the *last* person in the world who would like graphic novels. Mrs. Troller was old. Not as old as my gram, but pretty close. How did she even know what a graphic novel was?

She turned to the class. "Speaking of vampires . . ."

For a second, she looked right at me. Did she *know*? Was she going to say, "We just happen to have one sitting right here! Tom Marks, stand up and turn into a bat!"

She didn't say that.

She said, "Did any of you know that there was a real man who was named Dracula?"

Nobody did.

Mrs. Troller went on. "His name was Vlad Dracula. He was a prince who lived in the 1400s and fought some battles in Transylvania. He was nicknamed Vlad the Impaler because he impaled his enemies on stakes. It was rumored that he drank their blood, but no one knows for sure."

Some of the class thought it was disgusting

and went "Ewwwww!" Some of them thought it was cool. I wanted her to talk about something else.

"The man who wrote the book titled *Dracula* was Bram Stoker. He used Vlad's name," she said as she sat on the edge of her desk. "Many characters in fiction are based on real people from history." She turned to Zeke. "How much of your graphic novel have you written?"

"Just the first chapter," said Zeke.

"Well, no more note passing," said Mrs. Troller, "but please bring in that first chapter tomorrow. I'd like to see it."

"Excellent!" said Zeke.

I looked over at him and gave him my "Are you crazy?!" look. He gave me a thumbs-up.

Now we had to write a graphic novel.

In Art class our assignment was to draw some flowers in a vase. Capri tried to help me, but my flowers ended up looking like baseball gloves with monkey faces. I caught her staring at my ears a couple of times.

Mr. Baker looked at my drawing and said, "That's a nice monkey face on a baseball glove."

He had liked my self-portrait yesterday, so I figured if I said, "That's the way I see flowers sometimes," he'd like this too.

He didn't.

"Unfortunately, Mr. Marks, that's not what we are drawing today. Try again."

I erased my drawing and started over. I looked at Capri's and tried to copy it. Then I got a great idea.

"Hey, Capri," I whispered. "You're a really good artist. Would you want to draw some pictures of a vampire for a graphic novel?"

Capri scrunched up her face and said, "Ew. I don't like vampires."

"Well . . . you don't have to like them, you just have to draw them."

She looked at my ears again. "I'll think about it."

27.

Superpowers

I ate lunch with Zeke in the cafeteria. We ordered
our food from the cafeteria lady who looked like
she had been working there for a hundred fifty
years and wasn't happy about it.

"I'll have The Works Pizza, with everything on
it," said Zeke.

I jabbed him in the ribs with my elbow and
whispered, "No garlic."

"Oh, sorry! Never mind. I'll have plain cheese
pizza."

She gave him his cheese pizza and said, "Next!"

"Could I have two hamburgers?" I asked. "Cooked very rare, please."

"We make our burgers one way," she said in a grouchy voice. "Well done." She shoved two hamburgers on my tray and turned to the person behind me. "Next!"

Zeke and I sat down at our table in the corner.

"I've got an awesome idea!" he said.

"What?" I asked, totally knowing it would be:

a)   *Ridiculous*
b)   *Impossible*
c)   *Crazy*
d)   *Not Make Any Sense*
e)   *All of the Above*

Zeke was bouncing up and down on his seat. "You can use your superpowers to solve crimes and take out bad guys!"

"Shhh!" I said, and lowered my voice. "I'm *not* a superhero."

Zeke took a big bite of pizza and talked in between chewing. "But—*chew, chew, chew*—you've got

powers—*chew, chew, chew*—so, you're *kind of*—*chew, chew, chew*—a superhero."

"We agreed to keep this a secret!" I hissed at him. "And I'm *not* going to be a superhero!"

Abel came walking up with his tray of food and said, "Pardon me? May I join you two gentlemen or are you saving seats again today?"

Before I could say anything, Zeke said, "Hey, Abel. We're not saving seats. Sit down."

Abel sat down next to me. "Did I hear you discussing superheroes?"

I tried to answer before Zeke said anything, but my mouth was full of food and he's just too fast.

"Yeah!" said Zeke. "There's an awesome new one called . . . Super Vampire-Werewolf-Zombie Man!"

"I haven't heard of that particular superhero," said Abel.

"You will!" said Zeke.

I gave Zeke the dirtiest look I had ever given him.

◦ ◦ ◦

Luckily, a water pipe broke before Phys Ed and it flooded the track, so I didn't have to run in the sun. I had planned to tell Coach Tinoco that I had contracted a rare disease the night before called sunitis. So, I had to wear dark glasses, long sleeves, pants, and a hat in the sun. I hoped he would believe me. But since the track was flooded, we played basketball inside the gym. A couple of times I jumped pretty high when I was shooting a basket. I felt like I could've jumped five times higher, but I didn't try too hard, so nobody would get suspicious.

School was almost over. On my way to last period, Choir class, I felt really tired. I was sort of shuffling down the hallway, dragging my feet, with my arms hanging down at my sides. A kid pushed me out of the way and said, "Move it, zombie!"

I almost laughed.

In Choir, Mr. Stockdale pulled me aside and said, "I certainly hope you're not going to howl today?"

"I won't. I promise." I said it loud enough so that Annie, who was standing nearby, would hear. We sang that song "What a Wonderful World," which is about how wonderful the world is, but my world didn't feel so wonderful anymore. Just before we finished, I had a slight urge to howl, but I bit my tongue so I wouldn't. I tasted a little blood in my mouth. That made me really thirsty.

I had to get some blood. Fast.

28.

The Evil Mad Scientist

As soon as I got home, I wanted to try Zeke's "squeezing blood out of a steak" idea. I found a piece of frozen beef rib steak in the freezer. I was just pulling it out when Mom walked in.

"What on *earth* are you doing, Tom?"

"Uh, I'm . . . just getting a little snack."

She laughed. "A *steak*? No. I don't think so." She took it away from me and put it back in the freezer.

"What's for dinner?" I said.

She winked. "It's a surprise."

It's never good when Mom winks or says something is a surprise. I'd have to sneak down later, after everybody went to sleep, and get the steak.

Mom handed me an apple. "Whose turn is it to take out the trash barrels?"

"Emma's," I said.

"No, it's not!" yelled Emma from the living room, where she was pretending to read a book. I had seen she had her phone behind the book and was texting Pari. "It's Tom's turn!"

"It's *your* turn!" I yelled. "I did it last week!"

"No, you didn't!" she yelled back.

"Emma, you are such a liar! I did it last week because *you* said you had a headache! *You* have to do it for the next *two* weeks!"

"Stop yelling!" yelled Mom, which I thought was pretty hypocritical.

Emma came into the kitchen, pretending to limp. "My ankle still *really* hurts from when Tom violently knocked me down this morning."

"You are *such* a faker!" I said.

"Okay, okay!" said Mom. "Tom, you take out the trash tonight. Emma, you will do it the next three times."

"All right," said Emma.

There was no way Emma was going to take the trash out for three weeks in a row. She was probably already thinking of excuses to get out of doing it:

"I'm allergic to trash!"

"I hurt my arm helping an old lady bring in ten bags of her groceries!"

"I have to go to Pari's house right now or the world will end!"

I went into the backyard, where Muffin barked at me and then hid behind a tree. I took the three trash barrels—*that Emma should have been taking out!*—to the curb. Professor Beiersdorfer was across the street taking his trash barrels out too. For some reason he has nine of them.

Why did one old man, who lived by himself, have that many barrels?

What was he throwing away?

And what had he been burying in his backyard the night before?

I wanted to ask him, but I couldn't, obviously, because he'd think I was spying on him, which was exactly what I'd been doing.

Professor Beiersdorfer wore big, thick black glasses and had short white hair and a beard. He always wore the same thing every day: a red sweater, white shirt, tie, dark pants, and black rubber boots.

I think he was from Germany or Switzerland or

Sweden or somewhere where they had castles and a lot of snow and accordions and cows with bells on their necks. He still had an accent even though he had been living here forever.

When Zeke and I were six years old, Emma told us, "Professor Beiersdorfer is an evil mad scientist. Don't let him catch you or he'll turn you into monster robots in his secret basement laboratory, so he can take over the world!"

We *totally* believed her.

After that I almost peed my pants every time I saw him. I'd run away and hide whenever he came out of his house. I used to lie awake at night in bed, terrified that he was going to sneak in through my window and take me to his secret lab. I had nightmares about him turning me and Zeke into monster robots. When Mom and Dad found out that Emma had told us he was a mad evil scientist, she got in a *lot of trouble*.

"It was worth it," she said.

Of course, Zeke was disappointed when he found out Professor Beiersdorfer *wasn't* an evil mad scientist. "Aw, man! I wanted to be a robot!"

◦ ◦ ◦

I put the first trash barrel by the curb, and Professor Beiersdorfer waved to me from across the street.

"Good evening, Thomas."

I waved back. "Hi, Professor."

"You are back in school, yes? How did it go?"

"It went okay."

"Well, if you are ever in need of any Science help, you know, of course, whose door to come knocking on, yes? I have an excellent laboratory in . . . my basement."

Even though I knew he wasn't an evil mad scientist, it still sounded a little scary when he said that. "Okay, Professor. Thanks. I will."

"Good!" He looked up at the sky. "There will be the full moon tonight. That means the earth is located directly between the sun and moon. Should be beautiful, yes?"

◦ ◦ ◦

I had a *ton* of homework to do, which was completely unfair on the second day of school. It was like the teachers were having a contest to see who could give the most homework. I could picture them sitting in the teachers' lounge, drinking big cups of coffee, and then one of them saying, "Hey! Let's all give a *ton* of homework tonight!"

"Yeah! Great idea!"

"I'll assign a thousand-word essay!"

"I'll assign a big Science project!"

"I'll make them study for a fifty-question quiz!"

"Five pages of Math problems!"

"Memorize the Declaration of Independence!"

"Read ten pages about the Louisiana Purchase!"

"I hate kids!"

"Me too!"

∘ ∘ ∘

I had barely finished my homework when Mom finally called us to dinner. I was *starving*.

Emma, Dad, and I sat down. Mom was standing at the head of the table, holding a big bowl with green stuff sticking out of it.

"I have an announcement to make!" she said, with a smile on her face.

I silently groaned to myself. Mom's announcements are *always* bad. She *never* had a good announcement. She never said anything like, "We're going to Disney World!"

Or: "We're getting a hundred-inch TV screen!"

Or: "We're going to put in a swimming pool!"

Or: "I won the lottery and I'm giving you each a million dollars!"

Or: "We're sending Emma away to Europe for a year!"

This time was no different.

"We're going to start eating healthier," she said. "I read a very interesting article last week, and from now on we're eating vegetarian."

"What?!" I said in a panic. "You mean, like no meat at all?"

"Yes, doofus," said Emma. "That's what vegetarian means."

Mom threw a cherry tomato at Emma's forehead. It bounced off and landed in her lap.

"Ow!" cried Emma. "That hurt!"

"A cherry tomato *cannot* hurt you," said Mom. "And don't call your brother a doofus."

Emma picked up the cherry tomato and popped it in her mouth. "But he is!"

Vegetarian? How could Mom do this to me? Her

son was a vam-wolf-zom. I needed meat! Lots of it! All the time!

"I'll give it a try," said Dad, patting his stomach. "Maybe I'll drop a few pounds."

"It's fine with me," said Emma. "I'm, like, practically a vegetarian already."

Emma always tells people she's a vegetarian, even though she eats hamburgers and chicken and fish. She just lies *all the time*.

I had to stop this from happening and I had to stop it quickly. "Uh . . . my Science teacher told us today that it was bad to be a vegetarian."

"He did?" said Mom as she started scooping out the vegetables from the bowl. "Why?"

"Because . . . because our bones need meat or . . . or they dissolve."

I had no idea what I was saying.

"Your Science teacher is crazy," said Emma. "Who do you have?"

"Mr. Prady."

"I had him. He *is* crazy. And he smells like corn dogs."

She was right. Mr. Prady did smell like corn dogs.

"Well," said Mom. "We're going to give it a try for at least a month."

I would be a *dead* vam-wolf-zom in about an

hour if I didn't get some meat. I was starving. *And I needed blood.* I hoped Mom hadn't thrown that steak away. I started to eat the vegetables and noodles and fruit and nuts that were supposed to be our so-called dinner.

"How did your report on werewolves go?" asked Mom.

I almost choked on the piece of broccoli I was forcing myself to swallow. Then I remembered that Zeke had told Mom we were doing a werewolf report when I was holding my bed up over my head last night.

"It—it turned out great," I said.

"I'd like to read it," said Mom.

"Me too," said Dad. "I love werewolves."

I pushed a mushroom around my plate with my fork. "Okay . . . when I get it back from my teacher, I'll bring it home."

After dinner, I called Zeke and told him that HE had to write a fake werewolf report—*all by himself*—as well as the first chapter of our vampire graphic novel, because they were both HIS dumb ideas!

"I already started the graphic novel!" he said. "It's excellent!"

I didn't care. I had to get some meat and some blood. Fast!

29.

Tasting Blood

Three long hours later, Mom, Dad, and Emma were upstairs in their bedrooms. I snuck downstairs to the kitchen. I defrosted the frozen steak in the microwave and then cooked it for one minute on each side. Zeke had sent me a video of how to make steak in a frying pan. For some crazy reason he also sent me a video of vampires square-dancing.

The zombie part of me wanted to just eat the whole thing, but the vampire part of me wanted the blood. I didn't know what the werewolf part

wanted. Chew on the bone? I decided I would squeeze the blood out first, drink it, and then eat the meat.

I ran up to my room with the meat wrapped in a paper towel in one hand and a glass in my other hand. I kicked the door with the back of my foot to close it as I went in. I called Zeke on speakerphone, because he said I *had* to call him when I did it, and then I held the steak over the glass and squeezed it.

"Is it working?" asked Zeke.

Some blood dripped out of the steak into the glass.

"Yeah," I said.

"How much blood did you get?"

"About one-quarter of the glass."

"Drink it!"

"Okay . . ."

I put the meat down and picked up the glass.

I slowly raised the glass to my lips.

"Here goes . . ."

I took a sip.

I swallowed.

"How does it taste?" asked Zeke.

"Awesome . . ." I said.

Okay, this may sound totally gross, but it was the most delicious drink I ever had in my life. I drank the rest.

Then I heard a creaking noise. I turned around and there was Emma, peeking through the crack of the door, that I had *almost* closed when I kicked it with my foot.

"Oh . . . my . . . God," she whispered.

She turned and ran. I jumped up out of my seat.

"Emma, wait!"

It was too late. She was already running (something she *never* does) down the hall toward Mom and Dad's room. Before I got to her, she had knocked on their door and Mom had said, "Come in."

Emma opened the door, just as I was coming up behind her. "Tom is drinking blood!"

Mom and Dad, who were reading in their bed, didn't say anything at first. Then they both started laughing.

"I'm not joking!" said Emma in a serious voice. "I just saw him squeeze blood out of a piece of meat into a glass and drink it."

Mom and Dad stopped laughing.

"Tom?" said Mom. "Is this true?"

They all stared at me.

I tried to think of a really clever reason why I was drinking blood.

A Science experiment?

The coach had said blood would make me stronger?

Zeke had dared me to do it?

They were all pretty lame.

How was I going to keep this a secret from them? I couldn't keep coming up with excuses and explanations. I couldn't keep lying and hiding and pretending and sneaking around forever. We lived in the same house. They were going to find out sooner or later.

I decided I had to tell them.

Everything.

30.

The Truth, the Whole Truth, and Nothing but the Truth

I made Mom, Dad, and Emma sit on the bed. I was standing up, facing them. I took a deep breath.

"Okay . . . I know you're not going to believe this. But I'm *not* making it up. I *promise*. . . . It all started at Gram's. I woke up in the morning and felt a bite on my—"

"How *long* is this going to take?" complained Emma. "I have to read two chapters in this stupid book about this stupid guy who turns into a stupid cockroach."

"Shush, Emma!" said Mom. "Go on, Tom."

"I felt a bite on my neck when I woke up," I said. "Gram thought it was a spider bite and I thought it was a—"

"*Get* to the good part!" said Emma.

Mom gave Emma her most serious face. "Stop. Interrupting. Now." She turned to me. "Go on, Tom. There will be no further interruptions from Emma unless she wants to take out the trash for the whole month."

I told them everything that happened at Gram's, on the drive home, at the gas station, at school, after school, and today. Emma pretended to fall asleep once and Mom pinched her.

Then I finally told them: "So . . . I'm a vampire . . . and a werewolf . . . and a zombie."

They didn't say anything. They just looked at me. Then, they looked at one another.

Mom smiled.

Dad started chuckling.

Emma started giggling.

"It's *not* funny!" I said.

For some reason this made them laugh harder.

"I'm *not* lying!" I yelled.

Now all three were in hysterics. They were falling on one another laughing, wiping tears from their eyes. I had never seen them laugh so hard in my entire life.

"I AM SERIOUS!" I screamed. That scared them a little. They stopped laughing.

"I'm sorry, Tom," said Mom. "Is this a story you're writing for school? It's very good—"

"No! It's not a story!"

"Is this a prank?" said Dad, smiling as he looked around the room. "Is Zeke hiding somewhere with a camera?"

Emma, who was in her pajamas, looked around the room suspiciously. "He'd better not be!"

"He's not!" I said.

"Is this, like, a desperate, pathetic cry for attention?" said Emma in her usual bored voice.

"No! I'm not kidding, I'm not lying, I'm not making this up, I promise. I know it sounds crazy and nutty and impossible—"

"Ya think?" said Emma, rolling her eyes.

"Listen to me! I just told you, that's why I wasn't in the photograph, why I can't see my reflection, why I have fangs, why my skin is pale, and why I'm hungry all the time."

Emma did a big fake yawn.

"Stop it, Emma," said Mom. Then she turned to me. "Tommy, you're a normal eleven-year-old. You have a vivid imagination. All your feelings of being different and strange are perfectly normal for a boy going through adolescence."

"I can prove it!" I said as I went to the door. "I have super hearing. Watch." I ran down to the other end of the hallway. "Whisper something!"

"What should we whisper?" yelled Dad.

"It doesn't matter!" I yelled back.

Emma leaned over to Mom and Dad and whispered, "Tom is insane and needs to be put in a mental institution."

"I am not insane!" I shouted from down the hall. "And I am not going into a mental institution!"

"You read my lips!" said Emma.

"No, I didn't! Cover your mouth with your hand and say something!"

Emma put her hand over her mouth and whispered, "Can I please go to my room and do my homework and you guys deal with Mr. Crazy Pants."

"I'm not Mr. Crazy Pants!" I said, walking back down the hall.

"I know what this is," said Mom. "I just read an interesting article about people with super hearing, it's called hyperacusis."

"It's not that!" I said, coming into their room. "Vampires and werewolves can hear *ten times* better than normal people."

"Okay, I am so over this!" said Emma, standing up. "Good night."

I pushed her back down on the bed.

"Hey!" she said.

"Don't move," I said.

"What are you doing?" said Mom.

"Just watch."

I bent down and reached under the bed, and then I picked it up, with all three of them on it.

"*Now* do you believe me?"

"Oh, no!" cried Mom. "You're taking steroids!"

"I am not taking steroids!"

"I know!" said Dad. "It's a magic trick! You put something under the bed. Y'know, I wanted to be a magician—"

"IT'S NOT A MAGIC TRICK!"

I put the bed down.

"Okay," said Emma, crossing her arms. "If you're a vampire, then turn into a bat."

Why did she have to ask me that?

"I can't do that. I haven't learned how, yet."

"Then I guess you need to get your butt to Vampire School," said Emma.

Dad was looking under the bed. "Where's the magic gizmo? I can't see it."

Emma stood up again. "Okay, I'm going to find a nice, not too expensive, mental institution we can put Tom in."

"I am NOT making this up!" I said.

Mom reached out and took my hand. "Tommy . . . honey, maybe we should call someone for you to talk to? Like a counselor or therapist."

"What do I have to do to make you believe me?" I asked.

Suddenly, I felt something weird on my arms. And then my legs. And then my face. I was tingling all over my body. I looked out the window at the full moon rising through the trees.

And that's when I turned into a werewolf for the first time.

31.

A Beast in the Bedroom

I felt little hairs popping up everywhere on my body. I pulled up my shirtsleeves and saw hair growing on my arms. I felt my muscles getting bigger. I didn't know how big I was going to get, so I unbuttoned my shirt really fast and took it off. It was a brand-new shirt and I knew Mom would kill me if it got torn.

The hair was a little gross, but the muscles on my arms were awesome. I was built! And I didn't have to go to a gym and lift weights every day for a year.

I touched my face. It was about 30 percent hairy. My ears felt a little bigger. I opened my mouth and felt my teeth. They were a bit bigger and sharper. I guess I didn't transform into a full-on werewolf, because I was only one-third of one.

I was really glad that I was the kind of werewolf that stood up on two legs, like a person. I didn't have to walk around on all fours.

Meanwhile, Mom had fainted straight back onto the bed.

Dad sat there, frozen like a statue, with a crazy smile on his face.

Emma looked like she was going to puke.

I tipped my head back and let out a big howl. It was even louder than the one I did in Choir. I don't know whether I howled because that's what werewolves do when they turn, or whether I was relieved because I knew that they would *have* to believe me now.

Mom opened her eyes and sat up. Dad unfroze and his crazy smile disappeared. Emma closed her mouth. I was really glad she didn't puke.

"*Now* do you believe me?"

They slowly nodded their heads.

"I'm . . . I'm sorry we didn't believe you," said Mom softly. It looked like she was going to cry, but she didn't; her eyes just got watery.

I shrugged.

Mom always tries to say something nice, even when bad stuff happens. I didn't think she could say anything nice this time, but she tried.

"Tom . . . your . . . uh . . . fur looks . . . very soft," she said, trying to smile.

I touched my arm. It *was* pretty soft.

"You want to touch it?" I said, and moved toward the bed. They all leaned back a little and looked worried. "Guys, I'm not going to hurt you."

Dad smiled. "Heh-heh. I know that."

I held out my arm, and Mom tentatively petted it.

"It is . . . very soft," she repeated.

Dad petted my arm too. "Wow. . . . It is. . . . Touch him, Emma."

"Ew! No way!" she said. "I don't want to touch some wild animal."

"He's *not* a wild animal," said Mom. "He's your brother."

"What's the difference?" said Emma.

"Look at his arms!" said Dad as he let out a sigh. "I used to have biceps like that."

"Honey, you *never* had biceps like that," said Mom.

"Yes, I did!" said Dad.

"Oh my God, you guys, what is *wrong* with

you?!" said Emma. "We've got a beast standing in front of us. He's got *claws*."

I looked down at my hands. I did have little claws at the end of my fingers. They looked sharp. I could do some serious damage with those.

"And look at his teeth!" said Emma. "And his ears! He is *totally* gross!"

"Stop that, right now, Emma!" said Mom. "Tom, you are a very handsome werewolf."

"Should we put some newspapers down?" said Emma. "I mean, seriously, he might not be housebroken."

"I'm not going to pee on the carpet!" I said.

"How do we know that?" said Emma. "Who knows *what* you're going to do?"

Mom looked like she might start crying, but she didn't. "Tom. . . . We want you to know, that even though you're . . . well . . . different now—"

"*Different?*" said Emma. "He's a monster mutant freak!"

Mom turned to Emma and glared at her. "Young lady, do *not* call your brother a monster mutant freak! Apologize to him or you will be in a world of trouble!"

Mom can be scary when she wants to be. Emma backed off. "Sor-ry."

"As I was saying," continued Mom. "Even

though you're a vampire and a werewolf and a zombie . . . you're our son and we will always love you."

I kind of knew she was going to say that, but it was still nice to hear.

My dad tried to make me feel better too. "You know, Tom, I wanted to be a vampire when I was your age. Dracula had a cool cape and a bunch of pretty women following him around."

Mom gave him a look, but Dad didn't see it and he kept talking.

"And I wouldn't have minded being a werewolf either! They're superstrong and they get to run around at night and scare people. And a zombie—" He stopped and shook his head. "No, I have to be honest, I never wanted to be a zombie. They're pretty disgusting."

Mom gave Dad some Major Stink Eye. "Your *son* is a zombie!"

"One-third zombie," I corrected her.

Emma figured it was safe to talk again. "Does anyone else know about this?"

"Just Zeke," I said. "And *he* believed me *right away*! I didn't have to turn into a werewolf to prove it!" I hoped this would make them feel bad, but it didn't.

"Of course he did!" said Emma. "You could tell

Zeke that you had turned into a cockroach and he'd believe you! Speaking of which"—she looked at her watch—"I still have to read two chapters of that stupid cockroach book tonight."

"Emma," said Mom, "I think the fact that your brother is a vampire-werewolf-zombie takes precedence over homework."

"Okay," said Emma. "But if I fail this class, I will not get into the college of my choice and get a good job, and you guys will have to support me for the rest of my life!"

Emma always makes everything about herself.

Dad let out a sigh. "Well . . . I guess these things happen."

"No, they don't!" I said. "Who do you know that's been bitten by a vampire, a werewolf, and a zombie?"

"Well . . . nobody that I personally know," said Dad.

Mom started pacing. "What should we do? Should we call somebody?"

"Who are we going to call?" I said. "The Vampire-Werewolf-Zombie hotline?"

"Here's what we're going to do," said Emma. "First. We need to tie it up in the basement."

"Do not call your brother 'it,'" said Mom.

"We can't let him run around wild and free!"

"We are *not* tying him up, Emma!"

"Okay, but if he runs around the neighborhood, biting and eating people, and sucking their blood, I am *totally* going to say, 'I told you so'!"

"He is *not* going to do that," said Dad. Then he turned to me. "Are you, Tom?"

"I don't know," I said, glaring at Emma. "I might bite some people who aren't nice to me."

Emma pointed her finger at me. "Do not even *think* about biting me!"

I decided to growl, just to freak her out.

"Thomas! Do not growl at your sister!" said Mom.

"I *swear*, if you try to bite me," said Emma, "I will kill you!"

"Stop it, you two!" said Mom.

Dad put his hand up to get everybody's attention. "Well actually, since Tom's a vampire and a zombie, I think he's one of the 'undead.' So, technically you *can't* kill him."

"Actually, you *can*," I said. "A wooden stake in the heart can kill a vampire, a silver bullet can kill a werewolf, and if you cut off a zombie's head or stick something in its brain you can kill them too."

"Do we have any wooden stakes in the garage?" asked Emma.

"EMMA!" yelled Mom. "That is *not* funny." She sat back down on the bed. "We need to calmly figure out what we're going to do."

"Maybe there's a special school we can send Tom to," said Emma. "One that's really, really, really far away."

Mom shook her head. "We are *not* sending Tom *anywhere*. He is going to stay here and go to school and do all the things any other eleven-year-old boy does."

"Mom," said Emma, "eleven-year-old boys do a lot of disgusting things, but they *don't* go around eating people and drinking their blood!"

Mom turned to me, looking a little worried. "Tom? You haven't eaten or bitten anybody, have you?"

"No," I said. "But speaking of eating, I am STARVING!"

32.

Carrot Boy

We all went down to the kitchen. I ate the steak and some fish sticks left over from before Mom decided we were vegetarians. Dad made some coffee, and Emma slouched in a chair with her I am so mad at everybody face.

Mom sat down and started tapping the table with her finger. "Now, Tom, I think you should stay home tomorrow, so we can make our plans."

Stay home from school? I liked that idea.

"I've got a plan," said Emma. "Let's donate Tom to some medical research place so they can dissect

him and do experiments. I bet they'll pay us a lot of
money. Hey! You could buy me a car!"

Mom glared at Emma. "You'd better be joking,
young lady."

"I am," said Emma. "But can we at least call a
place to see how much they'd pay us?"

Mom ignored her and went on. "Now, let's not tell *anyone* about this, until we've figured out exactly what we are going to do."

"Don't tell Lucas Barrington!" I said to Emma. She gave me a look like she was going to come over and bite *me*.

"Who is Lucas Barrington?" asked Mom.

"Is that Carrot Boy?" asked Dad. "The kid who looked like a carrot and used to mow our lawn?"

"He does NOT look like a carrot!" said Emma. "He's cool looking."

Mom smiled at Emma. "Does someone have a new boyfriend?"

"No!" said Emma, The Queen of Liars. "Even if he *was* my boyfriend, he'd probably break up with me now because of Tom! Oh my God! No one is going to want to be friends with me anymore! Thanks a lot, Tom. You just totally ruined my life!"

Emma got up and stomped out of the room.

Mom reached across the table and patted my hand. Or was it my paw?

"She doesn't mean that, Tom."

Who was Mom kidding? Of course Emma meant it.

○ ○ ○

We called Gram to tell her what had happened. She thought it was a joke at first too. It was hard to convince her. We tried to show her what I looked like, as a werewolf, on the phone doing FaceTime. It didn't work. It was just like when Mom took a picture of Emma and me with her phone on the first day of school. It turns out you can't take a picture or a video of a vampire. It's because they're not really human or they're undead or have no soul or something.

Mom got on the phone and got really serious and said, "Mother, I swear on Dad's grave, this is real."

Then I got on and I promised and swore to her that we weren't making it up. That convinced her. Gram cried a little bit and said, "It's all my fault."

"No, it's not, Gram," I said.

"Yes, it is. You were with me when you got bitten," she said. "You were *my* responsibility." Her voice got soft. "Are you . . . are you ever going to come visit me again?"

"Of course I am, Gram."

But I wasn't so sure about that. Who knew what else was up in those woods waiting to bite me?

"We'll get through this, Tommy," said Gram. "And if there's anything I can do to help, and I mean *anything*, you just call me. Anytime. Twenty-four hours a day, three hundred sixty-five days a year, and three hundred sixty-six on leap year. If things get too hard for you down there, and you want to come stay with me for a while, you can."

"Thanks, Gram."

o o o

It was really late, almost midnight, when everybody finally went to bed. That was when I decided to scare Emma. If I *had* to be a vam-wolf-zom, I deserved to have fun. And Emma deserved it for all the times she had scared me when I was little. Besides telling me that Professor Beiersdorfer was an evil mad scientist she had also:

1. Put a creepy-looking, life-sized doll of hers in my bed when I was asleep, with a bloody knife in its hand. I woke up and found it staring at me.
2. Told me the world was going to blow up at midnight on New Year's Eve, right before all the firecrackers and fireworks went off.
3. Hidden in my closet and jumped out screaming at me, about a million times.
4. Hidden under my bed and made growling noises just before I fell asleep.
5. Put on a scary witch mask and chased me around the house.

Emma *totally* deserved to be scared.

I made my way down the dark hallway to her door. Our house is pretty old and has keyholes on the doorknobs that you can look through, so I bent down and peeked through the keyhole into Emma's room.

She had all her lights on and had propped her chair up against the door, so you couldn't open it. Did she forget that I could *easily* smash down her door? But I knew that Dad would get mad if I did, and I'd have to pay for a new one. I didn't have very much money, because Zeke had just convinced me to buy a super-lame video game called *Rabbit Attack!* It was The Worst Video Game Ever Invented. It was just rabbits throwing carrots at each other and then eating them.

Why do I listen to Zeke?

As I peeked through the keyhole, I could see Emma, asleep in bed, with her mouth open. I couldn't tell if she was drooling or not, but I bet she was.

She was holding my old T-ball baseball bat in one hand. In her other hand she was holding one of those garden stakes that my mom ties to newly planted trees so they grow straight. It was made of plastic, so it wouldn't work on a vampire. Emma is so lame.

She had also taped some garlic to her headboard She wasn't taking any chances. But then, I thought to myself, if *she* had turned into a vam-wolf-zom, I would've done the same thing.

I heard a squeaking noise. It was Emma's pet mouse, Terrence, running on his wheel, in his cage on her dresser. All of a sudden, he stopped running and looked at the door. It felt like he was looking right at me, through the keyhole.

I decided not to scare Emma. Plus, she did have garlic on her bed and I didn't want to get sick. And I was pretty tired. I could do it some other night. I was going to be a vam-wolf-zom for a long, long time.

33.

Meat, Sunglasses,
and Sunscreen

When I woke up the next morning I wasn't a werewolf anymore, which was a relief. Mom made me a ginormous breakfast: pancakes, eggs, bacon, toast, and cereal. She was tired because she had stayed up late, reading about vampires and werewolves and zombies on her iPad.

Dad called his boss and told him he had to take a personal day, so he wouldn't have to go to work.

"I didn't sleep at all last night!" complained Emma. (Another one of her gazillion lies. I *saw* her asleep.) "I thought Tom was going to come in and eat me."

"I wouldn't eat you if you were the last piece of food on earth!" I said.

"Quiet, you two!" said Mom. "Emma, raise your right hand."

"What? Why?"

Mom grabbed Emma's right hand and raised it up in the air. "Repeat after me: I swear I will NOT tell a single soul, not even Pari or Carrot Boy—"

"His name is not Carrot Boy!"

"Sorry," said Mom. "I mean, Lucas—about Tom."

Emma rolled her eyes. "I swear I will not tell anybody about my lame, crazy, gross, weirdo brother who let himself get bit by a vampire, werewolf, and zombie!"

On her way out the door, Emma yelled, "I'm going to look for a new family to adopt me!"

○ ○ ○

Dad went to the supermarket and bought a lot of meat for me. Mom said I didn't have to be a vegetarian, which was awesome. Dad also bought me some extra sunglasses and a whole case of sunscreen. There were, like, a hundred tubes

in a big box. He got me a couple of new hats too. I told him to get plain ones with no pictures or words.

When Emma got home from school and saw all the stuff Dad had bought me, she got mad.

"Hey! I want some new hats and sunglasses too!"

"You don't burn up in the sun," I said.

She made her usual pouty face. "That is *so* unfair!"

Then, Dad handed me a brand-new cell phone.

"Here, Tom. This is to be used *only* in case of emergency."

I seriously thought Emma was going to explode. "Oh my God! Are you kidding me?! You didn't give me a phone until I turned sixteen! He's only eleven!"

"Excuse me?" said Mom. "Did a vampire and werewolf and zombie bite you when you were eleven?"

"No!" she said. "But . . . but if I knew you would've given me a phone, I wish they would have!"

○ ○ ○

After talking about it for hours, Mom and Dad decided that we would go to school the next day and tell everybody what happened at a special assembly. That way we'd get it over with all at once. I wasn't so sure about the plan, but I agreed to do it as long as I didn't have to say anything.

"Emma?" said Mom. "Do you want to be at the assembly too?"

"Are you kidding me?!" she said. "No. Way. I will be hiding in a deep, dark hole!"

Mom and Dad called Principal Gonzales on the phone. They also called Mayor Lao, who my mom went to college with. They asked them both to come over to our house at exactly four thirty, to see something that was "extremely important" to the school and the community. They didn't tell them on the phone that I was a vam-wolf-zom. They wanted them to see me turn into a werewolf in person, so they wouldn't think we were crazy.

○ ○ ○

Principal Gonzales is tall and thin and has a lot of hair and smiles a lot. It was really weird seeing him in our living room. Mayor Lao is medium height and has short, dark hair. She was wearing a suit like the one Abel wore on the first day of school. Mayor Lao looked more like a spy than a mayor.

They sat down on our sofa. Emma was lurking around the corner at the dining room table, pretending she was doing homework. Mom and Dad launched into the whole story. Principal Gonzales smiled and Mayor Lao kept looking at her watch. You could tell they didn't believe any of it.

And then the sun went down.

When I turned into a werewolf, Principal Gonzales started breathing really fast. I thought he was going to hyperventilate and pass out.

Mayor Lao kept saying, "OhmyGod!OhmyGod! OhmyGod!OhmyGod!"

I lifted the sofa up, with both of them on it, to show how strong I was. That was *my* idea.

So we convinced them we weren't crazy. My parents told them their idea about having an assembly the next day at school.

Principal Gonzales said, "Sounds good to me. I'll arrange it."

Mayor Lao said, "I'll call the local TV news people to broadcast the assembly, so the whole town can be aware of Tom too."

As soon as Emma heard that, she practically

ran into the living room and said, "Mom? Dad? I have thought long and hard about this situation, and I believe with all my heart that I should be at the assembly with Tom, to support my dear brother at this very important moment in his life."

It looked like she even had some tears in her eyes. I have to admit, she can be a pretty good actress when she wants to be.

Then she said to Mom, "Do you think I should wear my new black dress or the red one I got for my birthday?"

Emma has absolutely no redeeming qualities.

○ ○ ○

Before I went to sleep, Mom came to my room and sat on my bed.

"Now, Tom, the first few days at school are going to be difficult, as people get used to you, but it'll get better. I promise."

My first two days of middle school hadn't exactly been easy—when everybody thought I was just a normal, boring kid. Now I had to go to school as a vam-wolf-zom.

How could it *ever* get better?

34.

This Is Not a Joke

They scheduled the assembly the next morning in the big auditorium. They didn't tell anybody what it was about. I waited offstage with Mom, Dad, and Emma, who kept adjusting her dress and combing her hair and looking at herself in a mirror. We could hear people get excited when they saw the TV cameras. I peeked out through the curtain. The whole school was there—all the teachers, students, cafeteria workers, even Grumpy Janitor, leaning against the wall, yawning.

Principal Gonzales came up to us and said, "Ready?"

Mom and Dad both looked at me, and I nodded.

Principal Gonzales went onstage by himself, tapped the microphone, and cleared his throat.

"Good morning," he said. "The motto of Hamilton Middle School is *Grata Sint Omnia*, which is Latin for 'All Are Welcome.' We believe in that motto one hundred percent here at Hamilton. All students are welcome. And that is what today's assembly is about. Something extraordinary has happened to one of your fellow students. You will not believe it. I didn't either, at first. But it is true."

He reached into his coat pocket and pulled out some pieces of paper that were stapled together. Mom and Dad had written a speech for him that explained most of the stuff that had happened to me. He started to read it. You could tell that people were confused at first. It was like when I told my parents and Emma. Some of them thought it was a joke, and Principal Gonzales had to tell everybody to be quiet a few times.

Then Mayor Lao came out and introduced me. I took a deep breath and walked onstage. The lights were really bright, so I couldn't see the audience very well, but I saw Zeke. He gave me two thumbs-up. I looked for Annie, but I couldn't see her. My

parents and Emma walked on behind me. Emma
smiled and waved at the TV cameras.

Unfortunately, I couldn't turn into a werewolf
because it wasn't nighttime. I had tried to turn
into a bat again, that morning, but I *still* couldn't
do it. Maybe I never would.

Principal Gonzales said, "Once again, this is
not a joke. This is not a prank. This is real. Tom
Marks is a vampire—"

I heard a girl in the front row whisper to her
friend, "Vampires are awesome!"

Maybe this wouldn't be such a bad thing?

Principal Gonzales went on, "*And* Tom is also a werewolf."

I heard the same girl whisper, "Werewolves are hot!"

This could be a *very* good thing.

Principal Gonzales added, "*And* Tom is also a zombie."

I heard the girl say, "Ew! Gross! Zombies are disgusting!"

It wasn't going to be a good thing.

Principal Gonzales pointed his finger at the audience. "Now, just like any other student here at Hamilton, Tom Marks is *not* to be made fun of or teased or called names or ridiculed . . . by *anyone*. Bullying is not what we do at Hamilton."

I just wanted this to be over. I was seriously thinking that I should move in with Gram. Or go to another school. Or run away. But where would I go?

Then, Principal Gonzales said, "Are there any questions?"

They turned the lights on in the auditorium, and about a million hands shot up.

"Can you turn into a bat?"

"How many people have you eaten?"

"Where is your cape?"

"Do you sleep in a coffin?"

"What do people taste like?"

"What are you going to be for Halloween?"

"Are you going to bite me?"

"Why can't you turn into a bat?"

"Can you howl?"

"Show us your fangs!"

"Are you going to eat anybody?"

"Are you going to start a zombie apocalypse?"

"What does blood taste like?"

"Can I get your autograph?"

"Can you bite me, just a little, so I turn into a vampire, but not a werewolf or a zombie?"

"My parents hired a magician for my birthday party this Saturday, but he can't come. Could you come instead?"

"Are you *sure* you can't turn into a bat?"

The bell rang.

Principal Gonzales said, "You are all dismissed to first period, and have a great day!"

Finally, it was over and I got off the stage. Emma smiled and bowed and waved at everybody. When we got backstage, Mom and Dad hugged me.

"I can pick you up from school today if you want," whispered Mom.

"No, thanks," I said. "I'll take the bus."

"Call us if there are any problems," said Dad.

How could there not be problems?

○ ○ ○

The first person I saw when I came out of the auditorium was Dog Hots.

"Dude!" he said. "Do something!"

"Like what?"

"I dunno." He shrugged. "Turn into a bat."

Why did *everyone* want me to turn into a bat?

"I can't turn into a bat," I said. "I just said that in the assembly about a million times."

"That sucks," said Dog Hots. "Hey? Can I bring some people over to your house tonight and watch you turn into a werewolf?"

"No!" I said.

Dog Hots walked away looking mad.

A girl came over and asked to take a selfie. I told her I wouldn't show up in the picture, but she took one anyway and then got mad when she couldn't see me.

Zeke came running up to me. "Awesome job, T-Man—I mean, Tom."

"I didn't do anything," I said.

"Hey! Check this out! It's gonna be excellent!" he said as he pulled out a notebook. It was the graphic novel he had started, the one he told Mrs. Troller about.

"Zeke, you don't need to do that anymore, everybody knows what I am now."

He didn't care.

"I call it *The All-New Awesome Adventures of Tim, The Vampire-Werewolf-Zombie*," said Zeke.

As I expected, the drawings were pretty bad. At least Tim didn't look anything like me. But he didn't look like a vam-wolf-zom either. He looked like a big, brown rabbit, with fangs and a pimple on his chin, wearing a cape. And for some reason he was carrying a banjo.

"Why does he have a banjo?" I asked.

"I love banjos!" said Zeke.

∘ ∘ ∘

When I walked down the hall, pretty much everybody moved out of the way and kept their distance. Some kids stared at me, some kids pretended not to stare at me, and some kids didn't look at all. Some whispered when I walked by, and a few looked scared.

I headed to my locker and saw Abel standing there. He was holding two different-colored

squares of carpet in his hands, looking back and forth between them. He had a blue suit on. How many suits did this kid have?

"Good morning, Mr. Marks," he said. "Do you prefer the brown carpet or the purple? I'm thinking of changing the color scheme and I want your input."

"Uh . . . I don't know."

Abel was acting like nothing had happened. Like it was just another day at school and his locker partner wasn't a vam-wolf-zom.

"Did you go to the assembly, Abel?"

"Yes, indeed. Sixteenth row, on the aisle, in the middle. Excellent view of the proceedings."

"So . . . you know what I am?"

"Of course." He nodded and held up the two carpet squares. "I'm unable to decide. I leave the verdict to you. Brown? Or purple?"

"I don't care. So, you don't mind that I'm a vampire-werewolf-zombie?"

"Everybody's got to be something," he said. "I'm one-third Irish, one-third Norwegian, and one-third Spanish. I thought you might be a vampire and possibly a werewolf when I shook your hand on our first day."

I suddenly remembered. On the first day of school, when we shook hands, Abel had said to me, "Your secret is safe with me."

Abel went on. "But I had no idea you were a zombie too. I do enjoy a good surprise now and then."

"And you don't mind sharing a locker with me?" I asked.

"Why on earth should I?" he said, putting the purple piece of carpet down at the bottom of the locker. "I'm going with the purple. Be seeing you! Hopefully at lunch?" He walked off, whistling.

I watched Abel go and I thought to myself, he wasn't The Weirdest Kid at School anymore. . . . *I* was.

Hands down.

No contest.

No competition.

And I would be the weirdest kid forever.

I put some books in the locker and noticed that Abel had written a new saying on the dry-erase board:

Whoever said that was not a vam-wolf-zom.

I walked down the hall to first period. When I turned the corner, Tanner Gantt was standing at the end of the hall.

I could tell he was waiting for me.

35.

To Beat Up or Not to Beat Up, That Is the Question

They had suspended Tanner Gantt for only two days for throwing me in the trash can. I would have suspended him for a whole week. As I walked toward him, I wondered what he had done on those two days at home. Did he sit around and watch TV and play video games and think about what he would do to me for revenge? Did he go to the swings in the park?

Some kids stopped to watch

as he walked up to me. I think he wanted to show everybody he wasn't afraid. I really hoped he wasn't going to ask me to turn into a bat.

"Oh noooo!" he said, pretending to be scared. "It's Terrifying Tom! I'm sooo scared!"

I didn't say anything. I just stood there, staring at him.

"What's the matter, freak?" he snarled as he pushed me against some lockers.

Some of the kids standing around us said, "Ooo," like kids usually do. You could tell they were hoping for a big fight.

"Bite him, Tom!"

"Suck his blood!"

"Claw him!"

"Eat him!"

"Turn into a bat!"

"Dude, he CAN'T turn into a bat!"

For a second, Tanner Gantt looked worried. Like I might actually do one of those things to him. I thought about giving him a mega-wedgie. I bet he'd never even had a regular wedgie his whole life.

What if I did bite him? Would he turn into a vam-wolf-zom? I didn't want to think about Tanner Gantt being really strong and fast and biting people. He'd love it.

"Move!" said a stern voice that I recognized right away. It was Ms. Heckroth, pushing through the crowd standing around us.

She turned and looked at them and said, "Get to class. Right now. Or you will all get lunch detention." She looked at Tanner Gantt and me. "You two stay here."

Everybody walked away. You could tell they were disappointed that there wasn't a fight.

Ms. Heckroth said, "Do you want to be suspended for an entire week, Mr. Gantt?"

"No, Ms. Heckroth," he said.

She turned to me. "Do *you* want to be suspended, Mr. Marks?"

Why was she asking me that? What had I done?

I was just standing there. Tanner Gantt was the one who had called *me* a freak.

"No, Ms. Heckroth," I said. "But, I wasn't—"

She didn't let me finish.

"Get to class."

As Tanner Gantt walked by me, he whispered, "Wimp."

∘ ∘ ∘

Mr. Kessler just nodded when I came in. During class, Annie sort of smiled at me but didn't say anything. A girl named Maren Nesmith, who sat right across from me, was staring me down like that snake did in Science class. Maren went to my old school and she hadn't liked me ever since I didn't dance with her in kindergarten because she had chocolate cake all over her dress.

She raised her hand. "Mr. Kessler, can I move to another seat?"

"Why?" he asked.

"Because Tom Marks is, like, staring at me, and it's, like, really creeping me out."

"I wasn't staring at you," I said. "*You* were staring at *me*."

"Mr. Kessler, I

totally think he wants to bite my neck and suck my blood," said Maren.

"Gross!" I said. "I don't want to bite your neck and suck your blood. That sounds disgusting."

All of a sudden Maren got super offended. "What?! *I'm* disgusting?! *My* neck is disgusting?!"

"Quiet, Maren," said Mr. Kessler. "Tom, are you going to bite Maren's neck and suck her blood?"

"No!" I said.

"Okay, Maren. You heard what Tom said. Stay in your seat."

"Excuse me, Mr. Kessler?" said Maren. "He may not want to suck my blood, but I've seen, like, a lot of zombie movies, and zombies, they just go crazy and, like, attack you without warning. I mean, you could just be talking to them, going, 'How's your day? What's up?' and then they go zombie crazy and take a big humongous bite out of you and then, like, you're a zombie, and that would be, like, so depressing. Can I *please* move to another seat?"

Mr. Kessler let out a big sigh. "Tom, are you going to try and eat Maren?"

"No!" I said, again.

"Okay. We're good," said Mr. Kessler as he opened up his *White Fang* book. "Now, who can tell me what happens when the character Bill goes off to find the sled dog that ran away?"

"He gets eaten by wolves," said Maren. "And I bet that's what Tom would like to do right now!"

Mr. Kessler let Maren move to a different seat.

○ ○ ○

In Science class, I could tell that Mr. Prady was afraid of me. His voice was a little higher than usual, but he tried to act brave. "Okay, Mr. Marks. Now, personally, I don't care if you're a vampire or a werewolf or a zombie or a mummy—"

A mummy? Why did he think I was a mummy?

"I don't care if you're a robot—"

I didn't look *anything* like a robot.

"I don't care if you're a kraken—"

How could he think I was a kraken? Did he even know what a kraken was? Krakens were giant sea monsters.

Mr. Prady kept talking.

"And I don't care if you're Frankenstein or the Invisible Man or King Kong or Predator or The Thing or the Phantom of the Opera or Godzilla or Bigfoot or the Creature from the Black Lagoon."

He was just showing off to the class that he knew a lot of monster names. Finally, he stopped. "In my class you will behave. You will do your work. No funny business."

"Yes, Mr. Prady," I said.

"Good. And just so you know, I'm not afraid of you."

He stayed behind his desk during the whole class.

o o o

I was more zombie-like at snack break. I was moving slowly, feeling kind of out of it, and all I wanted to do was eat. It seemed like sometimes I would feel more zombie than vampire or more werewolf than zombie or whatever.

Everybody kept their distance, except Abel.

"I've made macarons," he said, opening his briefcase. "Are you an aficionado?"

They were little white cookies that tasted amazing. I ate five.

o o o

In History class, Mrs. Troller acted nervous and smiled every time she looked at me. I was glad she didn't try to compare me to some historical event, like "Five million years ago, in the prehistoric period, we have the earliest recorded evidence of a werewolf, when a caveman named Urg drew a picture of a half-wolf-half-man on a cave wall."

∘ ∘ ∘

In Math class, Ms. Heckroth came up to my desk and handed me a stack of papers. "Here is the work we did in class yesterday and a pop quiz and the homework I assigned when you were absent. I expect it all to be done by the end of class."

I had hoped she'd give me a break since I was a vam-wolf-zom. She didn't.

∘ ∘ ∘

In Art class, Mr. Baker let us draw anything we wanted. I drew Muffin. The face wasn't too bad, but his body looked like a table. Capri didn't say anything to me the whole period. At least she wasn't looking at my ears, and I don't think she's ever going to call me Elfy. Juan Villalobos drew a picture of a wolf, in a cape, eating a boy who was

screaming, "Don't eat me Tom!" Mr. Baker took it away and sent him to the principal's office. I have to admit, it was a pretty good picture.

⚬ ⚬ ⚬

I didn't want to sit in the cafeteria and have everybody staring at me while I ate lunch. So, I decided to go eat by myself in one of the bathrooms. Zeke had told me he saw a kid do that on YouTube once. I went in the last stall, closed the door, and locked it. I would not recommend having your lunch in a bathroom stall. You're eating in a place where you usually do something else. It's uncomfortable, depressing, and gross.

I had almost finished with my lunch when I heard some guys come in.

"Man, can you freakin' believe it!"

"That is so messed up!"

"How could someone be so dumb to get bit by *three* things in one day!"

"*You're* that dumb, dude!"

Some of them laughed. I recognized a few of the voices, but not all of them.

"I wouldn't let a wolf bite me." It was Jason Gruber.

"Yeah, right. You're gonna fight off a wolf?"

"No, but I would've run away."

"Dude, you can't run faster than a wolf!"

"Yeah, but I can run faster than a zombie!"

"Where's he gonna get his blood?"

"He'll just buy some."

"Where? At the 7-Eleven? Gimme a Blood Slurpee, please!"

They laughed again.

"Man, if I was him, I'd go live in the woods or something."

"That sucks that he can't turn into a bat and fly."

"I sit next to him in Choir, I hope he doesn't bite me."

"Maren Nesmith said he wanted to bite her."

"I'd like to bite Maren Nesmith!"

They laughed *again*.

"Seriously, I'm gonna keep a wooden stake in my locker."

"I'm gonna bring some garlic to school."

"I wanna see him turn into a wolf."

The door to the bathroom opened and I heard someone else come in.

"Hey, Abel, nice suit!"

"You share your locker with Marks, don't you?"

"It figures they'd have the two weirdest kids share a locker."

"Dude, seriously, what's up with the suits?" said a kid whose voice I didn't recognize.

"He's a freak. He wears a suit every day. Since like third grade."

"Why do you wear a suit to school, weirdo?"

Abel cleared his throat and said, "For the same reason, I assume, that you gentlemen prefer to adorn yourself in blue jeans, T-shirts with a logo or image or some pop culture item, and what appears to be the exact same style of running shoe. You enjoy the way it looks."

They laughed at him.

"Why do you talk like that for, Abel?"

"Yeah, seriously, what is *wrong* with you?"

"Gentlemen, lunch period is almost over," said Abel. "I'm sure none of us wishes to get detention by being tardy to sixth period. I suggest you let me conclude my business here, and I will depart."

"Yeah?" said the kid who sounded older. "What if we're not through with you?"

I peeked through the crack in the stall door. They were circling around Abel. What were they going to do to him? Some of them were pretty big. Should I run out and get a teacher? Should I yell? And then I remembered something.

I was a vam-wolf-zom.

I unlocked the stall door, opened it, and came out.

36.

Another Plan

They were all surprised to see me.

"Whoa!"

"It's him!"

"Wh-what are you doing in here?"

First, I just stared at them. Then, I turned to the biggest guy and said, "The next person who says something to Abel about the way he talks, or what he wears, or does *anything* to him . . . I will rip their throat out."

Then I smiled, showing off my fangs.

They all ran out of the bathroom, practically

knocking one another over as they went through the door.

The biggest guy yelled over his shoulder, "We're telling the principal, Marks! They're gonna suspend you!"

Abel turned to me and smiled. "Thank you, Mr. Marks."

I shrugged. "Being a vam-wolf-zom has gotta be good for something."

"I am quite certain you will discover it has many positive uses. Question: Would you actually rip someone's throat out?"

"No," I said. "It sounds gross. Do you think they're going to tell anybody I said that?"

Abel stroked his chin. "I don't believe so. If they did, they might get in trouble too, if the two of us relayed to the authorities what occurred here. However, there is no accounting for riff-raff such as they."

Abel did talk weird, but this wasn't the time to bring that up.

"Just so you know, Mr. Marks, I could have taken care of myself," he said.

What? Was Abel kidding? There were five guys. Two of them were huge.

He smiled. "I am somewhat skilled in the martial arts. I have a black belt in karate."

I laughed. I couldn't help it. Abel Sherrill looked like the last person in the world who could do karate, let alone get a black belt.

"I see you have doubts," he said. "Perfectly understandable. Allow me to demonstrate."

He put down his briefcase, took a stance, jumped up in the air, flipped over, and did a flying kick that sent a trash can across the room, putting a dent in it. He landed on his feet like a cat. He adjusted his jacket, straightened his tie, picked up his briefcase, and smiled.

∘ ∘ ∘

I left the bathroom, making a note to never get on Abel's bad side.

I was still worried about those guys telling on me. They could lie and make up some crazy story. Would I get suspended? Would I get expelled? I had promised Principal Gonzales I wouldn't do anything like that at school.

Maybe telling everyone I was a vam-wolf-zom was a huge mistake. Should I have kept it a secret? My teachers were either afraid of me or felt sorry for me or pretended to be super nice. All the kids stared at me and gave me weird looks and whispered that I was going to eat them.

I decided I didn't want to go to school at Hamilton anymore.

I had a new plan: *The Run Away and Live Somewhere Else Plan.*

o o o

I thought about living up in the hills behind our house. We had a tent and sleeping bags and some camping equipment that my dad had borrowed from Gram and forgotten to return.

But I don't like camping.

My family tried it once, and it was fun for about an hour. Then bugs started biting us and it got freezing and my dad couldn't start a fire, so we couldn't cook hot dogs or roast marshmallows, and we had to eat cereal for dinner—with no milk, because Mom forgot to bring it. Then it rained, and the tent leaked and collapsed on top of us, and my dad said a lot of swear words and my mom yelled at him for swearing and we ended up sleeping in our car and my dad snored all night.

In the morning, Emma said, "I am going to sue you guys for cruel and unusual treatment of children."

That was the last time my family ever went camping.

o o o

Then I remembered that there was an old, empty cabin up in the woods, near Gram's house. We had hiked up there once. It was grungy, but I could clean it up. It had a fireplace. It was near a stream, so I could get water. I could totally live there.

I decided that I'd leave a letter, telling Mom and Dad that I was going away. Emma would *love* the news. She'd probably have a party. I started walking toward the gate to the school parking lot, where I could sneak out. I was thinking about what I would write in the letter.

Dear Mom and Dad,

I have decided to go live in the woods by myself. I'll come visit you on my birthday and Christmas and Mother's Day and Father's Day. I'll miss you. Tell Emma that I won't miss her.

"Hey, Tom!"

I turned around, and there was Annie. We hadn't said anything to each other all day.

"Hey," I said.

"I didn't see you at lunch."

"Yeah. I-I had to go do something."

"Oh."

I was only about five feet from the gate to the parking lot.

"Where are you going?" she asked.

"I-I was going to my locker."

"Isn't your locker back that way?" she said, pointing behind her to where my locker actually was.

"Oh, yeah. I forgot."

We didn't say anything for a bit. We just stood there.

Finally, she said, "I'm sorry you got bit by all those things."

"Yeah," I said. "Me too."

I wanted to say goodbye to her, but I didn't want anybody to know I was going.

What if I *never* saw her again, though? I was going to live in a cold, dirty cabin in the woods. And take baths in a freezing river. I'd have to use leaves for toilet paper. And eat birds and rabbits and squirrels and chipmunks. *The Run Away and Live in a Cabin in the Woods Plan* wasn't sounding so great anymore.

"Can I ask you something?" said Annie.

I *knew* she was going to ask about bats or blood or eating people.

I sighed and answered, "Sure."

"Do you want to be in a band I'm starting?"

37.

The Eight Words No One Wants to Hear

Annie Barstow wanted me to be in her band.

"Yeah. Sure," I said, trying to sound cool, but I knew she could tell I was excited.

"I like your voice," said Annie.

"Thanks. I like your voice too."

"Thanks."

"You're a good singer," I said.

"Thanks. You're a good singer too."

"Thanks."

We sounded just as dumb as Emma and Carrot Boy.

"Just don't howl anymore." She smiled.

"I promise I won't howl anymore."

Earlier, I would have rated this day a 3, but now it was a 9.

"Cool. I'll tell everybody else," she said.

Wait.

What did she mean *everybody else?* There were *other* people in the band? For some reason I had thought it was going to be a two-person band. Just me and Annie.

"Who else is in the band?"

"Well, so far, it's just me and that girl Capri. She plays piano. She said you're in her Art class."

Capri's in the band? Why does Capri have to be in the band? I didn't want Capri in the band.

"Cool," I said.

Annie went on. "And Dog Hots—I mean Landon. He plays drums."

Landon!

Right. *That* was Dog Hots' real name. But I didn't want Dog Hots in the band either.

"And Abel Sherrill," said Annie.

This wasn't a band, this was an orchestra.

"Abel Sherrill?" I said. "Seriously?"

"Yeah," she said. "I had no idea he was such an awesome guitar player."

Abel was an awesome guitarist on top of being a black belt in karate? And he can make amazing food? What else could he do? Scuba dive? Fly a helicopter? Build a rocket? Read minds?

Annie went on. "And Zeke said he'd be our roadie. You know, carry our equipment, help us set stuff up, keep all the fans away." She laughed. I did too. It was the first time I had laughed in a while.

"We better get to sixth period," she said. "See ya."

"See ya."

I watched her walk away. I was starting to get used to her short hair.

∘ ∘ ∘

I was dressing for Phys Ed when Coach Tinoco walked up and said the eight words that nobody wants to hear in middle school: "You need to go to the principal's office."

38.

Zero Tolerance

I was sitting across from Principal Gonzales, who had his hands folded on top of his desk. He wasn't smiling.

"Tom? Did you threaten to tear someone's throat out?"

I thought for a second and then I said, "No, sir."

"Jason Gruber says you did."

"Well, to be completely accurate, I didn't say 'tear'; I said 'rip.'"

Principal Gonzales sat back in his chair and crossed his arms. "And why did you say that?"

"Jason and some other guys were bothering somebody."

"Who?"

"Abel Sherrill."

"Is he a friend of yours?"

"No. We just share a locker."

"What did Jason and the other boys do to Abel? Did they hit him?"

"No."

"Did they threaten to do something physical to him?"

"No."

"You threatened to do something to the other boys," said Principal Gonzales, leaning forward. "We can't have you doing that, Tom."

"I wasn't going to really do it. I just wanted to—"

He held up his hand. "We have a zero-tolerance bullying policy here at Hamilton. I have to suspend you."

My parents were going to kill me.

"For how long?" I asked.

"The rest of today and Friday. Now, I understand, this hasn't been an easy week for you. I know how you feel."

How did he know how I felt? Had he been bitten by a vampire and a werewolf and a zombie and then have to start middle school *the next day*? I really wanted to say that, but I didn't.

Principal Gonzales folded his hands on his desk again. "But you can come back Monday and have a fresh start."

"What about Jason Gruber and those other kids?" I said. "Are you going to suspend them too?"

He didn't say anything right away. Then he looked out the window. "Their actions don't warrant suspension under our school guidelines."

Life is so not fair.

Mom came to pick me up. She looked serious when she walked into the office. Principal Gonzales told her what happened, and she just sat there nodding her head. Afterward, I went to my locker to get my books, so I could do my homework while I was suspended. At least I finally remembered my locker combination.

Mom and I walked toward the parking lot. We passed by the Phys Ed field, and I saw Tanner Gantt watching us. Two days ago, I had seen *his* mom take *him* home when he got suspended, and now he was seeing my mom do the same thing.

Life is so freaking weird sometimes.

"T-Man!" yelled Zeke, running up to the fence. "I heard you beat up twenty guys in the bathroom! And threw Jason Gruber through a window! And stuffed a kid in the toilet! And got expelled! And you might go to jail!"

"No, Zeke." I sighed. "None of that happened."

"It didn't?" he said disappointedly. "Aw, man."

My mom said hi to Zeke and went ahead to the car.

"I did get suspended," I said.

Zeke got excited again.

"Excellent! I'll get suspended too, so we can work on you turning into a bat and flying! How should I get suspended—I know! I can cheat on a test! I'll ask Coach Tinoco to give me a test right now so I can cheat on it. How do you cheat in Phys Ed? Or I could destroy school property! Do you think I could break this fence? What if—"

"Stop!" I said. "*Don't* get suspended. I'll call you later."

"Zimmerman!" yelled Coach Tinoco from across the field. "Get away from that fence. Get over here and give me fifty jumping jacks! Now!"

"Excellent!" said Zeke as he happily ran over and started doing jumping jacks.

ooo

When we got in the car, Mom turned to me and said, "I'm very proud of you for coming to Abel's defense, Tom."

Phew. I thought she was going to be really mad.

"But, let's not threaten to rip anybody's throat out again, okay?"

"Okay. I won't," I said.

"Hungry?"

"I'm *always* hungry, Mom. I'm a zombie."

"How does a rare cheeseburger sound?"

"Excellent," I said. "But three sounds better."

39.

A Visitor

The Worst First Four Days of Middle School That Ever Happened to Any Kid in the History of the World were over.

Mom and Dad decided we should go up to Gram's for the weekend, to get away for a few days.

"No way I am going up there!" said Emma. "I'll get bit by a vampire or a werewolf or a zombie or ALL of the above!"

"You're going," said Mom.

"You can't make me!" protested Emma.

"That's true, we can't," said Dad. Then he smiled. "But Tom can."

Emma looked mad, terrified, and confused at the same time. "What?!"

"I'm kidding!" said Dad, laughing.

"That is NOT funny!" said Emma.

She went to Gram's.

°°°

As we pulled up to her house, Emma grabbed Muffin and bolted out of the car before it stopped, kissed Gram on the cheek as she ran past her at the door, went inside, and announced, "I am never leaving this house the whole weekend!"

Gram hugged me even harder than Mom did.

"I'm barbecuing spare ribs for dinner," she said. "Nice and rare for you."

I looked over at her neighbor's yard. Stuart was back from the vet. He had a patch over his left eye. He trotted up to the fence and looked up at me. But he didn't bark. He lowered his head and lay down. I went over and petted him for the first time. He had soft fur too.

Gram hugged me about a million more times and asked a ton of questions, including if I could turn into a bat and fly.

"No. Sorry. I tried."

She looked a little disappointed, but then she said, "Well, it might be an acquired skill. Or maybe you need somebody to teach you."

After dinner—I ate twelve ribs—Dad made a fire in the fireplace. We sat in the living room, drank hot chocolate with lots of whipped cream, and ate s'mores.

"You want to watch a scary movie?" asked Gram.

"No!" said Emma, giving me a dirty look. "I'm living in

a scary movie, I don't want to watch one!"

Emma picked the movie. It was a stupid romantic one that she watches once a week. After about five minutes, Mom looked out the window and jumped up off the sofa.

"Wait! The moon's coming out! Emma, pause the movie so Gram can see Tom turn into a werewolf."

"No! This is the best part!" complained Emma. "Gram can see him do it tomorrow night."

"Actually, she can't," said Dad. "The last full moon of the month is tonight."

"Oh my God," said Emma. "Our whole lives are going to revolve around Tom now, aren't they?"

Gram winked at me. "Em, if you'd been bitten, I'd want to see you turn into a werewolf."

So would I. But, maybe not. Emma would be the *worst* vam-wolf-zom ever. She would complain twenty-four hours a day. Just the fact that she couldn't see herself in a mirror would make her go crazy. Or at least crazier than she already is. I don't even want to think about it.

"Gram, trust me," said Emma, "you do *not* want to see Tom turn into a werewolf. He gets hairy all

over, his nose turns into a snout, he gets paws and claws and this gnarly underbite—"

Gram held up her hand to stop Emma from talking, which is not easy to do. "I've seen a lot of werewolf movies. I have a pretty good idea of what happens."

"Those are movies!" said Emma. "This is real!"

I hated to admit it, but Emma was right for once. Would Gram freak out?

Emma did her fake serious face. "Gram, it is so gross and disgusting and, you know, at your age, you might not be able to handle it."

Gram smiled. "I lived through the sixties. I can handle it."

So, we paused the movie. The hair started growing all over me and I felt my arms getting bigger. Gram stared as I transformed, and quietly said, "Wow . . . Wow . . . Wow. . . ."

Emma texted Carrot Boy on her phone the whole time, but looked up every once in a while to say, "Yuck!" and "Ew! and "Why is this happening to *me*?!"

For some reason Mom and Dad held hands the whole time I changed. I don't know why.

"Tom, can you speed it up?" said Emma. "I want to watch my movie sometime in the next year!"

"Zip it, Emma!" said Gram. She's the only person who can get Emma to shut up.

Finally, I was done. Gram leaned back and slowly shook her head.

"Well, I've seen a lot of trippy things in my life, but that beats them all. Never thought I'd watch my grandson turn into a werewolf, but I guess life is full of surprises. You make a fine werewolf, Tommy. I wish your grandpa could've seen this. He loved werewolves. I'm more particular to zombies."

I think Gram is the only person in the world who likes zombies. Except maybe other zombies. I looked out the window at the moon and howled, because you sort of have to do that when you're a werewolf.

"That is one great howl," said Gram.

Stuart, the dog next door, howled back from outside. It was weird, it almost sounded like he was saying "Hello."

Gram reached out and touched my face. "You kind of look like my great-uncle Archie. He had a thick beard and a lot of hair on his arms. He was one hairy guy."

Emma looked like she was going to have a stroke. "Wait—could he have been a werewolf, too? Do werewolves run in the family? Is there some deep, dark family secret no one has told me about? Why am I in this family?!"

"Calm down, Em," said Gram. "Does it hurt when you change, Tommy?"

"No, not really," I said. "The hair actually kind of tickles."

"Okay!" said Emma. "The wolfman show is over. Can we go back to the movie?"

I had this weird urge to jump out the window and run around in the woods, but I didn't. We watched the rest of the movie. Emma cried at the end, like she always does, and then I went to bed.

∘ ∘ ∘

I had turned off the light in my bedroom and was just closing the window when I heard a noise coming from outside. I cocked my head toward the sound, so I could hear better. It was coming from the woods.

I looked out and noticed something flying above the trees, off in the distance. It was tiny and dark colored, and coming toward the house. When it got closer, I could see what it was. A small brown bat, with black wings, flying right at me. It stopped flapping its wings, glided in, and landed on the windowsill. The bat was about four inches tall, with big ears and tiny black eyes.

It looked up at me.

And smiled.

I swear.

It *really, honestly, truly* smiled.

And then it opened its mouth and said, "May I come in?"

Acknowledgments

These people deserve special thanks.

Kiev Richman for hearing an early version of this book and whose enthusiastic reaction inspired me to keep writing!

Jud Laghi, my agent, who did not give up.

Richard Abate, who heard my idea for the book, had great suggestions, and introduced me to Jud Laghi.

Sally Morgridge, a wise and patient editor, who made this book so much better.

Mark Fearing, for the cool illustrations.

John Simko, copyeditor, for his meticulous work.

Doug McGrath, my advisor, concierge, unpaid therapist, and buddy.

Annette Banks, M.A. Education, Occidental College, teacher, for reading and rereading and rereading numerous drafts of this book and giving honest, intelligent, helpful notes (and for marrying me).

My parents, who took me to the library and let me buy books at the school book sales.

You, the person reading this right now. Keep reading!